Marx Machiavelli Chesterton Emerson Joyce
Abbott Hardy Montaigne Cooper Austen
Defoe Melville Haggard Hugo
Christie Eliot Grimm
Stoker Carroll Molière
Wilde Maupassant Byron
Engels Schiller
Garnett Einstein Fitzgerald Smith
Hawthorne Kafka
Goethe Dostoyevsky Hall
Cotton
Baum Kipling Doyle Willis
Leslie Dumas Henry Nietzsche
Flaubert Turgenev Balzac
Stockton Vatsyayana Crane
Burroughs Whitman Verne
Curtis Tocqueville Gogol Vinci
Homer Widger Tolstoy Busch
Darwin Thoreau
Potter Freud Zola Twain Plato Scott
Lawrence
Kant Jowett Stevenson Dickens
Andersen Burton Hesse Harte
London Descartes Cervantes
Poe Aristotle Wells Voltaire
Hale James Hastings
Cooke
Bunner Shakespeare
Richter Chekhov Chambers Irving
da Shaw Wodehouse Benedict
Doré Swift Dante Alcott
Pushkin
Newton

tredition®

tredition was established in 2006 by Sandra Latusseck and Soenke Schulz. Based in Hamburg, Germany, tredition offers publishing solutions to authors and publishing houses, combined with worldwide distribution of printed and digital book content. tredition is uniquely positioned to enable authors and publishing houses to create books on their own terms and without conventional manufacturing risks.

For more information please visit: www.tredition.com

TREDITION CLASSICS

This book is part of the TREDITION CLASSICS series. The creators of this series are united by passion for literature and driven by the intention of making all public domain books available in printed format again - worldwide. Most TREDITION CLASSICS titles have been out of print and off the bookstore shelves for decades. At tredition we believe that a great book never goes out of style and that its value is eternal. Several mostly non-profit literature projects provide content to tredition. To support their good work, tredition donates a portion of the proceeds from each sold copy. As a reader of a TREDITION CLASSICS book, you support our mission to save many of the amazing works of world literature from oblivion. See all available books at www.tredition.com.

Project Gutenberg

The content for this book has been graciously provided by Project Gutenberg. Project Gutenberg is a non-profit organization founded by Michael Hart in 1971 at the University of Illinois. The mission of Project Gutenberg is simple: To encourage the creation and distribution of eBooks. Project Gutenberg is the first and largest collection of public domain eBooks.

Boy Life Stories and Readings Selected From The Works of William Dean Howells

William Dean Howells

Imprint

This book is part of TREDITION CLASSICS

Author: William Dean Howells
Cover design: Buchgut, Berlin – Germany

Publisher: tredition GmbH, Hamburg - Germany
ISBN: 978-3-8472-1573-8

www.tredition.com
www.tredition.de

The intention of the TREDITION CLASSICS series is to make world literature in the public domain available in printed format. Literary enthusiasts and organizations, such as Project Gutenberg, world-wide have scanned and digitally edited the original texts. tredition has subsequently formatted and redesigned the content into a modern reading layout. Therefore, we cannot guarantee the exact reproduction of the original format of a particular historic edition. Please also note that no modifications have been made to the spelling, therefore it may differ from the orthography used today.

BOY LIFE
W. D. HOWELLS

KITE-TIME

BOY LIFE

STORIES AND READINGS SELECTED FROM THE WORKS OF

WILLIAM DEAN HOWELLS

AND ARRANGED FOR SUPPLEMENTARY READING IN ELEMENTARY SCHOOLS BY

PERCIVAL CHUBB

DIRECTOR OF ENGLISH IN THE ETHICAL CULTURE SCHOOL, NEW YORK

ILLUSTRATED

HARPER & BROTHERS PUBLISHERS

NEW YORK AND LONDON
MCMIX

HARPER'S MODERN SERIES

OF SUPPLEMENTARY READERS FOR THE ELEMENTARY SCHOOLS

Each, Illustrated, 16mo, 50 Cents School.

BOY LIFE

Stories and Readings Selected from the Works of William Dean Howells, and Arranged by Percival Chubb, Director of English in the Ethical Culture School, New York.

"The literary culture which we are trying to give our boys and girls is not sufficiently contemporaneous, and it is not sufficiently national and American....

"Among the living writers there is no one whose work has a more distinctively American savor than that of William Dean Howells.... The juvenile books of Mr. Howells' contain some of the very best pages ever written for the enjoyment of young people."—Percival Chubb.

(*Others in Preparation.*)

HARPER & BROTHERS, PUBLISHERS, NEW YORK

Published September, 1909.

INTRODUCTION

There are two conspicuous faults in the literary culture which we are trying to give to our boys and girls in our elementary and secondary schools: it is not sufficiently contemporaneous, and it is not sufficiently national and American. Hence it lacks vitality and actuality. So little of it is carried over into life because so little of it is interpretative of the life that is. It is associated too exclusively in the child's mind with things dead and gone—with the Puritan world of Miles Standish, the Revolutionary days of Paul Revere, the Dutch epoch of Rip Van Winkle; or with not even this comparatively recent national interest, it takes the child back to the strange folk of the days of King Arthur and King Robert of Sicily, of Ivanhoe and the Ancient Mariner. Thus when the child leaves school his literary studies do not connect helpfully with those forms of literature with which—if he reads at all—he is most likely to be concerned: the short story, the sketch, and the popular essay of the magazines and [Pg x] newspapers; the new novel, or the plays which he may see at the theatre. He has not been interested in the writers of his own time, and has never been put in the way of the best contemporary fiction. Hence the ineffectualness and wastefulness of much of our school work: it does not lead forward into the life of to-day, nor help the young to judge intelligently of the popular books which later on will compete for their favor.

To be sure, not a little of the material used in our elementary schools is drawn from Longfellow, Whittier, and Holmes, from Irving and Hawthorne; but because it is often studied in a so-called thorough and, therefore, very deadly way—slowly and laboriously for drill, rather than briskly for pleasure—there is comparatively little of it read, and almost no sense gained of its being part of a national literature. In the high school, owing to the unfortunate domination of the college entrance requirements, the situation is not much better. Our students leave with a scant and hurried glimpse—if any glimpse at all—of Emerson, Thoreau, and Whitman, or of Lowell, Lanier, and Poe; with no intimate view of Hawthorne, our great classic; none at all of Parkman and Fiske, our historians; or of writers like Howells, James, and Cable, or Wilkins, Jewett, and Deland, and a worthy company of story-tellers. [Pg xi]

We may well be on our guard against a vaunting nationalism. It retards our culture. There should be no confusion of the second-rate values of most of our American products with the supreme values of the greatest British classics. We may work, of course, toward an ultimate appreciation of these greatest things. We fail, however, in securing such appreciation because we have failed to enlist those forms of interest which vitalize and stimulate literary studies—above all, the patriotic or national interest. Concord and Cambridge should be dearer, as they are nearer, to the young American than even Stratford and Abbotsford; Hawthorne should be as familiar as Goldsmith; and Emerson, as Addison or Burke. Ordinarily it is not so; and we suffer the consequences in the failure of our youth to grasp the spiritual ideals and the distinctively American democratic spirit which find expression in the greatest work of our literary masters, Emerson and Whitman, Lowell and Lanier. Our culture and our nationalism both suffer thereby. Our literature suffers also, because we have not an instructed and interested public to encourage excellence.

Among the living writers there is no one whose work has a more distinctively American savor than that of William Dean Howells; and it is to make his delightful writings more widely [Pg xii] known and more easily accessible that this volume of selections from his books for the young has been prepared as a reading-book for the elementary school. These juvenile books of Mr. Howells contain some of the very best pages ever written for the enjoyment of young people. His two books for boys—*A Boy's Town* and *The Flight of Pony Baker*—rank with such favorites as *Tom Sawyer* and *The Story of a Bad Boy*.

These should be introductory to the best of Mr. Howells' novels and essays in the high school; for Mr. Howells, it need scarcely be said, is one of our few masters of style: his style is as individual and distinguished as it is felicitous and delicate. More important still, from the educational point of view, he is one of our most modern writers: the spiritual issues and social problems of our age, which our older high-school pupils are anxious to deal with, are alive in his books. Our young people should know his *Rise of Silas Lapham* and *A Hazard of New Fortunes*, as well as his social and literary criticism. As stimulating and alluring a volume of selections may be made for high-school students as this volume will be, we venture to predict, for the younger boys and girls of the elementary school.

In this little book of readings we have made, we believe, an entirely legitimate and desirable use of the books named above. *A Boy's Town* [Pg xiii] is a series of detachable pictures and episodes into which the boy—or the healthy girl who loves boys' books—may dip, as the selections here given will, we believe, tempt him to do. The same is true of *The Flight of Pony Baker*. The volume is for class-room enjoyment; for happy hours of profitable reading—profitable, because happy. Much of it should be read aloud rather than silently, and dramatic justice be done to the scenes and conversations which have dramatic quality.

Percival Chubb.

I

ADVENTURES IN A BOY'S TOWN

[Pg 3]

HOW PONY BAKER CAME PRETTY NEAR RUNNING OFF WITH A CIRCUS

Just before the circus came, about the end of July, something happened that made Pony mean to run off more than anything that ever was. His father and mother were coming home from a walk, in the evening; it was so hot nobody could stay in the house, and just as they were coming to the front steps Pony stole up behind them and tossed a snowball which he had got out of the garden at his mother, just for fun. The flower struck her very softly on her hair, for she had no bonnet on, and she gave a jump and a hollo that made Pony laugh; and then she caught him by the arm and boxed his ears.

"Oh, my goodness! It was you, was it, you good-for-nothing boy? I thought it was a bat!" she said, and she broke out crying and ran into the house, and would not mind his father, who was calling after her, "Lucy, Lucy, my dear child!" [Pg 4]

Pony was crying, too, for he did not intend to frighten his mother, and when she took his fun as if he had done something wicked he did not know what to think. He stole off to bed, and he lay there crying in the dark and expecting that she would come to him, as she always did, to have him say that he was sorry when he had been wicked, or to tell him that she was sorry when she thought she had not been quite fair with him. But she did not come, and after a good while his father came and said: "Are you awake, Pony? I am sorry your mother misunderstood your fun. But you mustn't mind it, dear boy. She's not well, and she's very nervous."

"I don't care!" Pony sobbed out. "She won't have a chance to touch me again!" For he had made up his mind to run off with the circus which was coming the next Tuesday.

He turned his face away, sobbing, and his father, after standing by his bed a moment, went away without saying anything but "Don't forget your prayers, Pony. You'll feel differently in the morning, I hope."

Pony fell asleep thinking how he would come back to the Boy's Town with the circus when he was grown up, and when he came out in the ring riding three horses bareback he would see his father and mother and sisters in one of the lower seats. They would not know him, but he would know them, and he would send for them to come to the dressing-room, and would be very good to them, all but his mother; he would be very cold and stiff with her, though he would know that she was prouder of him than all the rest put together, and she would go away almost crying. [Pg 5]

HE BEGAN BEING COLD AND STIFF WITH HER THE VERY NEXT MORNING

[Pg 7]

He began being cold and stiff with her the very next morning, although she was better than ever to him, and gave him waffles for breakfast with unsalted butter, and tried to pet him up. That whole day she kept trying to do things for him, but he would scarcely speak to her; and at night she came to him and said, "What makes you act so strangely, Pony? Are you offended with your mother?"

"Yes, I am!" said Pony, haughtily, and he twitched away from where she was sitting on the side of his bed, leaning over him.

"On account of last night, Pony?" she asked, softly.

"I reckon you know well enough," said Pony, and he tried to be disgusted with her for being such a hypocrite, but he had to set his teeth hard, hard, or he would have broken down crying.

"If it's for that, you mustn't, Pony dear. You don't know how you frightened me. When your snowball hit me, I felt sure it was a bat, and I'm so afraid of bats, you know. I didn't [Pg 8] mean to hurt my poor boy's feelings so, and you mustn't mind it any more, Pony."

She stooped down and kissed him on the forehead, but he did not move or say anything; only, after that he felt more forgiving toward his mother. He made up his mind to be good to her along with the rest when he came back with the circus. But still he meant to run off with the circus. He did not see how he could do anything else, for he had told all the boys that day that he was going to do it; and when they just laughed, and said, "Oh yes. Think you can fool your grandmother! It'll be like running off with the Indians," Pony wagged his head, and said they would see whether it would or not, and offered to bet them what they dared.

The morning of the circus day all the fellows went out to the corporation line to meet the circus procession. There were ladies and knights, the first thing, riding on spotted horses; and then a band-chariot, all made up of swans and dragons. There were about twenty baggage-wagons; but before you got to them there was the greatest thing of all. It was a chariot drawn by twelve Shetland ponies, and it was shaped like a big shell, and around in the bottom of the shell there were little circus actors, boys and girls, dressed in their circus clothes, and they all looked exactly like fairies. They scarce [Pg 9] seemed to see the fellows, as they ran alongside of their chariot, but Hen Billard and Archy Hawkins, who were always cutting up, got close enough to throw some peanuts to the circus boys, and some of the little circus girls laughed, and the driver looked around and cracked his whip at the fellows, and they all had to get out of the way then.

Jim Leonard said that the circus boys and girls were all stolen, and nobody was allowed to come close to them for fear they would try to send word to their friends. Some of the fellows did not believe it, and wanted to know how he knew it; and he said he read it in a paper; after that nobody could deny it. But he said that if you went with the circus men of your own free will they would treat you first-rate; only they would give you burnt brandy to keep you little; nothing else but burnt brandy would do it, but that would do it, sure.

Pony was scared at first when he heard that most of the circus fellows were stolen, but he thought if he went of his own accord he would be all right. Still, he did not feel so much like running off with the circus as he did before the circus came. He asked Jim Leonard whether the circus men made all the children drink burnt brandy; and Archy Hawkins and Hen Billard heard him ask, and began to mock him. They [Pg 10] took him up between them, one by his arms and the other by the legs, and ran along with him, and kept saying, "Does it want to be a great big circus actor? Then it shall, so it shall," and, "We'll tell the circus men to be very careful of you, Pony dear!" till Pony wriggled himself loose and began to stone them.

After that they had to let him alone, for when a fellow began to stone you in the Boy's Town you had to let him alone, unless you were going to whip him, and the fellows only wanted to have a little fun with Pony. But what they did made him all the more resolved to run away with the circus, just to show them.

He helped to carry water for the circus men's horses, along with the boys who earned their admission that way. He had no need to do it, because his father was going to take him in, anyway; but Jim Leonard said it was the only way to get acquainted with the circus men. Still, Pony was afraid to speak to them, and he would not have said a word to any of them if it had not been for one of them speaking to him first, when he saw him come lugging a great pail of water, and bending far over on the right to balance it.

"That's right," the circus man said to Pony. "If you ever fell into that bucket you'd drown, sure." [Pg 11]

He was a big fellow, with funny eyes, and he had a white bulldog at his heels; and all the fellows said he was the one who guarded the outside of the tent when the circus began, and kept the boys from hooking in under the curtain.

Even then Pony would not have had the courage to say anything, but Jim Leonard was just behind him with another bucket of water, and he spoke up for him. "He wants to go with the circus."

They both set down their buckets, and Pony felt himself turning pale when the circus man came toward them. "Wants to go with the circus, heigh? Let's have a look at you." He took Pony by the shoulders and turned him slowly round, and looked at his nice clothes, and took him by the chin. "Orphan?" he asked.

Pony did not know what to say, but Jim Leonard nodded; perhaps he did not know what to say, either; but Pony felt as if they had both told a lie.

"Parents living?" The circus man looked at Pony, and Pony had to say that they were.

He gasped out, "Yes," so that you could scarcely hear him, and the circus man said:

"Well, that's right. When we take an orphan, we want to have his parents living, so that we can go and ask them what sort of a boy he is." [Pg 12]

He looked at Pony in such a friendly, smiling way that Pony took courage to ask him whether they would want him to drink burnt brandy.

"What for?"

"To keep me little."

"Oh, I see." The circus man took off his hat and rubbed his forehead with a silk handkerchief, which he threw into the top of his hat before he put it on again. "No, I don't know as we will. We're rather short of giants just now. How would you like to drink a glass of elephant milk every morning and grow into an eight-footer?"

Pony said he didn't know whether he would like to be quite so big; and then the circus man said perhaps he would rather go for an

India-rubber man; that was what they called the contortionists in those days.

"Let's feel of you again." The circus man took hold of Pony and felt his joints. "You're put together pretty tight; but I reckon we could make you do if you'd let us take you apart with a screw-driver and limber up the pieces with rattlesnake oil. Wouldn't like it, heigh? Well, let me see!" The circus man thought a moment, and then he said: "How would double-somersaults on four horses bare-back do?"

Pony said that would do, and then the circus man said: "Well, then, we've just hit it, because [Pg 13] our double-somersault, four-horse bareback is just going to leave us, and we want a new one right away. Now, there's more than one way of joining a circus, but the best way is to wait on your front steps with your things all packed up, and the procession comes along at about one o'clock in the morning and picks you up. Which 'd you rather do?"

Pony pushed his toe into the turf, as he always did when he was ashamed, but he made out to say he would rather wait out on the front steps.

"Well, then, that's all settled," said the circus man. "We'll be along," and he was going away with his dog, but Tim Leonard called after him:

"You hain't asked him whereabouts he lives?"

The circus man kept on, and he said, without looking around, "Oh, that's all right. We've got somebody that looks after that."

"It's the magician," Jim Leonard whispered to Pony, and they walked away.

THE CIRCUS MAGICIAN

A crowd of the fellows had been waiting to know what the boys had been talking about to the circus man, but Jim Leonard said, "Don't you tell, Pony Baker!" and he started to run, [Pg 14] and that made Pony run, too, and they both ran till they got away from the fellows.

"You have got to keep it a secret; for if a lot of fellows find it out the constable'll get to know it, and he'll be watching out around the corner of your house, and when the procession comes along and he sees you're really going he'll take you up, and keep you in jail till your father comes and bails you out. Now, you mind!"

Pony said, "Oh, I won't tell anybody," and when Jim Leonard said that if a circus man was to feel *him* over, that way, and act so kind of pleasant and friendly, he would be too proud to speak to anybody, Pony confessed that he knew it was a great thing all the time.

"The way'll be," said Jim Leonard, "to keep in with him, and he'll keep the others from picking on you; they'll be afraid to, on account of his dog. You'll see, he'll be the one to come for you to-night; and if the constable is there the dog won't let him touch you. I never thought of that."

Perhaps on account of thinking of it now Jim Leonard felt free to tell the other fellows how Pony was going to run off, for when a crowd of them came along he told them. They said it was splendid, and they said that if they could make their mothers let them, or if they could get out of the house without their mothers knowing [Pg 15] it, they were going to sit up with Pony and watch out for the procession, and bid him good-bye.

At dinner-time he found out that his father was going to take him and all his sisters to the circus, and his father and mother were so nice to him, asking him about the procession and everything, that his heart ached at the thought of running away from home and leaving them. But now he had to do it; the circus man was coming for him, and he could not back out; he did not know what would happen if he did. It seemed to him as if his mother had done everything she could to make it harder for him. She had stewed chicken for dinner, with plenty of gravy, and hot biscuits to sop in, and peach preserves afterward; and she kept helping him to more, because she said boys that followed the circus around got dreadfully hungry. The eating seemed to keep his heart down; it was trying to get into his throat all the time; and he knew that she was being good to him, but if he had not known it he would have believed his mother was just doing it to mock him.

Pony had to go to the circus with his father and sisters, and to get on his shoes and a clean collar. But a crowd of the fellows were there at the tent door to watch out whether the circus man would say anything to him when he went in; and Jim Leonard rubbed against him, when [Pg 16] the man passed with his dog and did not even look at Pony, and said: "He's just pretending. He don't want your father to know. He'll be round for you, sure. I saw him kind of smile to one of the other circus men."

It was a splendid circus, and there were more things than Pony ever saw in a circus before. But instead of hating to have it over, it seemed to him that it would never come to an end. He kept thinking and thinking, and wondering whether he would like to be a circus actor; and when the one came out who rode four horses bareback and stood on his head on the last horse, and drove with the reins in his teeth, Pony thought that he never could learn to do it; and if he could not learn he did not know what the circus men would say to him. It seemed to him that it was very strange he had not told that circus man that he didn't know whether he could do it or not; but he had not, and now it was too late.

A boy came around calling lemonade, and Pony's father bought some for each of the children, but Pony could hardly taste his.

"What is the matter with you, Pony? Are you sick?" his father asked.

"No. I don't care for any; that's all. I'm well," said Pony; but he felt very miserable.

After supper Jim Leonard came round and went up to Pony's room with him to help him [Pg 17] pack, and he was so gay about it and said he only wished *he* was going, that Pony cheered up a little. Jim had brought a large square of checked gingham that he said he did not believe his mother would ever want, and that he would tell her he had taken if she asked for it. He said it would be the very thing for Pony to carry his clothes in, for it was light and strong and would hold a lot. He helped Pony to choose his things out of his bureau drawers: a pair of stockings and a pair of white pantaloons and a blue roundabout, and a collar, and two handkerchiefs. That was all he said Pony would need, because he would have his circus clothes right away, and there was no use taking things that he would never wear.

Jim did these up in the square of gingham, and he tied it across cater-cornered twice, in double knots, and showed Pony how he could put his hand through and carry it just as easy. He hid it under the bed for him, and he told Pony that if he was in Pony's place he should go to bed right away or pretty soon, so that nobody would think anything, and maybe he could get some sleep before he got up and went down to wait on the front steps for the circus to come along. He promised to be there with the other boys and keep them from fooling or making a noise, or doing anything to wake his father up, [Pg 18] or make the constable come. "You see, Pony," he said, "if you can run off this year, and come back with the circus next year, then a whole lot of fellows can run off. Don't you see that?"

Pony said he saw that, but he said he wished some of the other fellows were going now, because he did not know any of the circus boys and he was afraid he might feel kind of lonesome. But Jim Leonard said he would soon get acquainted, and, anyway, a year would go before he knew it, and then if the other fellows could get off he would have plenty of company.

As soon as Jim Leonard was gone Pony undressed and got into bed. He was not sleepy, but he thought maybe it would be just as well to rest a little while before the circus procession came along for him; and, anyway, he could not bear to go down-stairs and be with the family when he was going to leave them so soon, and not come back for a whole year.

After a good while, or about the time he usually came in from playing, he heard his mother saying: "Where in the world is Pony? Has he come in yet? Have you seen him, girls? Pony! Pony!" she called.

But somehow Pony could not get his voice up out of his throat; he wanted to answer her, but he could not speak. He heard her say, "Go out to the front steps, girls, and see if you can [Pg 19] see him," and then he heard her coming up the stairs; and she came into his room, and when she saw him lying there in bed, she said: "Why, I believe in my heart the child's asleep! Pony! Are you awake?"

Pony made out to say no, and his mother said: "My! what a fright you gave me! Why didn't you answer me? Are you sick, Pony? Your father said you didn't seem well at the circus; and you didn't eat any supper, hardly."

Pony said he was first-rate, but he spoke very low, and his mother came up and sat down on the side of his bed.

"What is the matter, child?" She bent over and felt his forehead. "No, you haven't got a bit of fever," she said, and she kissed him, and began to tumble his short black hair in the way she had, and she got one of his hands between her two, and kept rubbing it. "But you've had a long, tiresome day, and that's why you've gone to bed, I suppose. But if you feel the least sick, Pony, I'll send for the doctor."

Pony said he was not sick at all; just tired; and that was true; he felt as if he never wanted to get up again.

His mother put her arm under his neck, and pressed her face close down to his, and said very low: "Pony dear, you don't feel hard toward your mother for what she did the other night?" [Pg 20]

He knew she meant boxing his ears, when he was not to blame, and he said: "Oh no," and then he threw his arms round her neck and cried; and she told him not to cry, and that she would never do such a thing again; but she was really so frightened she did not know what she was doing.

When he quieted down, she said: "Now say your prayers, Pony, 'Our Father,'" and she said, "Our Father" all through with him, and after that, "Now I lay me," just as when he was a very little fellow. After they had finished she stooped over and kissed him again, and when he turned his face into his pillow she kept smoothing his hair with her hand for about a minute. Then she went away.

Pony could hear them stirring about for a good while downstairs. His father came in from uptown at last, and asked: "Has Pony come in?"

And his mother said; "Yes, he's up in bed. I wouldn't disturb him, Henry. He's asleep by this time."

His father said: "I don't know what to make of the boy. If he keeps on acting so strangely I shall have the doctor see him in the morning."

Pony felt dreadfully to think how far away from them he should be in the morning, and he would have given anything if he could have gone down to his father and mother and told [Pg 21] them what he was going to do. But it did not seem as if he could.

By-and-by he began to be sleepy, and then he dozed off, but he thought it was hardly a minute before he heard the circus band, and knew that the procession was coming for him. He jumped out of bed and put on his things as fast as he could; but his roundabout had only one sleeve to it, somehow, and he had to button the lower buttons of his trousers to keep it on. He got his bundle and stole down to the front door without seeming to touch his feet to anything, and when he got out on the front steps he saw the circus magician coming along. By that time the music had stopped and Pony could not see any procession. The magician had on a tall, peaked hat, like a witch. He took up the whole street, he was so wide in the black glazed gown that hung from his arms when he stretched them out, for he seemed to be groping along that way, with his wand in one hand, like a blind man.

He kept saying in a kind of deep, shaking voice, "It's all glory; it's all glory," and the sound of those words froze Pony's blood. He tried to get back into the house again, so that the magician should not find him, but when he felt for the door-knob there was no door there anywhere; nothing but a smooth wall. Then he sat down on the steps and tried to shrink up so [Pg 22] little that the magician would miss him; but he saw his wide goggles getting nearer and nearer; and then his father and the doctor were standing by him looking down at him, and the doctor said:

"He has been walking in his sleep; he must be bled," and he got out his lancet, when Pony heard his mother calling: "Pony, Pony! What's the matter? Have you got the nightmare?" and he woke up, and found it was just morning.

The sun was shining in at his window, and it made him so glad to think that by this time the circus was far away and he was not with it, that he hardly knew what to do.

He was not very well for two or three days afterward, and his mother let him stay out of school to see whether he was really going to be sick or not. When he went back most of the fellows had forgotten that he had been going to run off with the circus. Some of them that happened to think of it plagued him a little and asked how he liked being a circus actor.

Hen Billard was the worst; he said he reckoned the circus magician got scared when he saw what a whaler Pony was, and told the circus men that they would have to get a new tent to hold him; and that was the reason why they didn't take him. Archy Hawkins said: "How long did you have to wait on the front steps, [Pg 23] Pony dear?" But after that he was pretty good to him, and said he reckoned they had better not any of them pretend that Pony had not tried to run off if they had not been up to see.

Pony himself could never be exactly sure whether he had waited on the front steps and seen the circus magician or not. Sometimes it seemed all of it like a dream, and sometimes only part of it. Jim Leonard tried to help him make it out, but they could not. He said it was a pity he had overslept himself, for if he had come to bid Pony good-bye, the way he said, then he could have told just how much of it was a dream and how much was not.

JIM LEONARD'S HAIR-BREADTH ESCAPE

Jim Leonard's stable used to stand on the flat near the river, and on a rise of ground above it stood Jim Leonard's log-cabin. The boys called it Jim Leonard's log-cabin, but it was really his mother's, and the stable was hers, too. It was a log stable, but up where the gable began the logs stopped, and it was weather-boarded the rest of the way, and the roof was shingled.

Jim Leonard said it was all logs once, and that the roof was loose clapboards, held down by logs that ran across them, like the roofs in [Pg 24] the early times, before there were shingles or nails, or anything, in the country. But none of the oldest boys had ever seen it like that, and you had to take Jim Leonard's word for it if you wanted to believe it. The little fellows nearly all did; but everybody said afterward it was a good thing for Jim Leonard that it was not that kind of roof when he had his hair-breadth escape on it. He said himself that he would not have cared if it had been; but that was when it was all over, and his mother had whipped him, and everything, and he was telling the boys about it.

He said that in his Pirate Book lots of fellows on rafts got to land when they were shipwrecked, and that the old-fashioned roof would have been just like a raft, anyway, and he could have steered it right across the river to Delorac's Island as easy! Pony Baker thought very likely he could, but Hen Billard said:

"Well, why didn't you do it, with the kind of a roof you had?"

Some of the boys mocked Jim Leonard; but a good many of them thought he could have done it if he could have got into the eddy that there was over by the island. If he could have landed there, once, he could have camped out and lived on fish till the river fell.

It was that spring, about fifty-four years ago, [Pg 25] when the freshet, which always came in the spring, was the worst that anybody could remember. The country above the Boy's Town was under water for miles and miles. The river-bottoms were flooded so that the corn had to be all planted over again when the water went down. The freshet tore away pieces of orchard, and apple-trees in bloom came sailing along with logs and fence-rails and chicken-coops, and pretty soon dead cows and horses. There was a dog chained to a dog-kennel that went by, howling awfully; the boys would have given anything if they could have saved him, but the yellow river whirled him out of sight behind the middle pier of the bridge, which everybody was watching from the bank, expecting it to go any minute. The water was up within four or five feet of the bridge, and the boys believed that if a good big log had come along and hit it, the bridge would have been knocked loose from its piers and carried down the river.

Perhaps it would, and perhaps it would not. The boys all ran to watch it as soon as school was out, and stayed till they had to go to supper. After supper some of their mothers let them come back and stay till bedtime, if they would promise to keep a full yard back from the edge of the bank. They could not be sure just how much a yard was, and they nearly all [Pg 26] sat down on the edge and let their legs hang over.

Jim Leonard was there, holloing and running up and down the bank, and showing the other boys things away out in the river that nobody else could see; he said he saw a man out there. He had not been to supper, and he had not been to school all day, which might have been the reason why he would rather stay with the men and watch the bridge than go home to supper; his mother would have been waiting for him with a sucker from the pear-tree. He told the boys that while they were gone he went out with one of the men on the bridge as far as the middle pier, and it shook like a leaf; he showed with his hand how it shook.

Jim Leonard was a fellow who believed he did all kinds of things that he would like to have done; and the big boys just laughed. That made Jim Leonard mad, and he said that as soon as the bridge began to go, he was going to run out on it and go with it; and then they would see whether he was a liar or not! They mocked him and danced round him till he cried. But Pony Baker, who had come with his father, believed that Jim Leonard would really have done it; and at any rate, he felt sorry for him when Jim cried.

He stayed later than any of the little fellows, because his father was with him, and even all the [Pg 27] big boys had gone home except Hen Billard, when Pony left Jim Leonard on the bank and stumbled sleepily away, with his hand in his father's.

When Pony was gone, Hen Billard said: "Well, going to stay all night, Jim?"

And Jim Leonard answered back, as cross as could be, "Yes, I am!" And he said the men who were sitting up to watch the bridge were going to give him some of their coffee, and that would keep him awake. But perhaps he thought this because he wanted some coffee so badly. He was awfully hungry, for he had not had anything since breakfast, except a piece of bread-and-butter that he got Pony Baker to bring him in his pocket when he came down from school at noon-time.

Hen Billard said, "Well, I suppose I won't see you any more, Jim; good-bye," and went away laughing; and after a while one of the men saw Jim Leonard hanging about, and asked him what he wanted there at that time of night; and Jim could not say he wanted coffee, and so there was nothing for him to do but go. There was nowhere for him to go but home, and he sneaked off in the dark.

When he came in sight of the cabin he could not tell whether he would rather have his mother waiting for him with a whipping and some supper, or get to bed somehow with neither. He climbed softly over the back fence and crept up to the [Pg 28] back door, but it was fast; then he crept round to the front door, and that was fast, too. There was no light in the house, and it was perfectly still.

All of a sudden it struck him that he could sleep in the stable-loft, and he thought what a fool he was not to have thought of it before. The notion brightened him up so that he got the gourd that hung beside the well-curb and took it out to the stable with him; for now he remembered that the cow would be there, unless she was in somebody's garden-patch or cornfield.

He noticed as he walked down toward the stable that the freshet had come up over the flat, and just before the door he had to wade. But he was in his bare feet, and he did not care; if he thought anything, he thought that his mother would not come out to milk till the water went down, and he would be safe till then from the whipping he must take, sooner or later, for playing hooky.

Sure enough, the old cow was in the stable, and she gave Jim Leonard a snort of welcome and then lowed anxiously. He fumbled through the dark to her side, and began to milk her. She had been milked only a few hours before, and so he got only a gourdful from her. But it was all strippings, and rich as cream, and it was smoking warm. It seemed to Jim Leonard that [Pg 29] it went down to his very toes when he poured it into his throat, and it made him feel so good that he did not know what to do.

There really was not anything for him to do but to climb up into the loft by the ladder in the corner of the stable, and lie down on the old last year's fodder. The rich, warm milk made Jim Leonard awfully sleepy, and he dropped off almost as soon as his head touched the cornstalks. The last thing he remembered was the hoarse roar of the freshet outside, and that was a lulling music in his ears.

The next thing he knew, and he hardly knew that, was a soft, jolting, sinking motion, first to one side and then to the other; then he seemed to be going down, down, straight down, and then to be drifting off into space. He rubbed his eyes and found it was full daylight, although it was the daylight of early morning; and while he lay looking out of the stable-loft window and trying to make out what it all meant, he felt a wash of cold water along his back, and his bed of fodder melted away under him and around him, and some loose planks of the loft floor swam weltering out of the window. Then he knew what had happened. The flood had stolen up while he slept, and sapped the walls of the stable; the logs had given way, one after another, and had let him down, with the roof, into the water. [Pg 30]

He got to his feet as well as he could, and floundered over the rising and falling boards to the window in the floating gable. One look outside showed him his mother's log-cabin safe on its rise of ground, and at the corner the old cow, that must have escaped through the stable door he had left open, and passed the night among the cabbages. She seemed to catch sight of Jim Leonard when he put his head out, and she lowed to him.

Jim Leonard did not stop to make any answer. He clambered out of the window and up onto the ridge of the roof, and there, in the company of a large gray rat, he set out on the strangest voyage a boy ever made. In a few moments the current swept him out into the middle of the river, and he was sailing down between his native shore on one side and Delorac's Island on the other.

All round him seethed and swirled the yellow flood in eddies and ripples, where drift of all sorts danced and raced. His vessel, such as it was, seemed seaworthy enough. It held securely together, fitting like a low, wide cup over the water, and perhaps finding some buoyancy from the air imprisoned in it above the window. But Jim Leonard was not satisfied, and so far from being proud of his adventure, he was frightened worse even than the rat which shared it. As soon as he could get his voice, he began to shout for help [Pg 31] to the houses on the empty shores, which seemed to fly backward on both sides while he lay still on the gulf that swashed around him, and tried to drown his voice before it swallowed him up. At the same time the bridge, which had looked so far off when he first saw it, was rushing swiftly toward him, and getting nearer and nearer.

He wondered what had become of all the people and all the boys. He thought that if he were safe there on shore he should not be sleeping in bed while somebody was out in the river on a roof, with nothing but a rat to care whether he got drowned or not.

Where was Hen Billard, that always made fun so; or Archy Hawkins, that pretended to be so good-natured; or Pony Baker, that seemed to like a fellow so much? He began to call for them by name: "Hen Billard—*O* Hen! Help, help! Archy Hawkins—*O* Archy! I'm drowning! Pony, Pony—*O* Pony! Don't you *see* me, Pony?"

He could see the top of Pony Baker's house, and he thought what a good, kind man Pony's father was. Surely *he* would try to save him; and Jim Leonard began to yell: "O Mr. Baker! Look here, Mr. Baker! It's Jim Leonard, and I'm floating down the river on a roof! Save me, Mr. Baker, save me! Help, help, somebody! Fire! Fire! Fire! Murder! Fire!" [Pg 32]

By this time he was about crazy, and did not half know what he was saying. Just in front of where Hen Billard's grandmother lived, on the street that ran along the top of the bank, the roof got caught in the branches of a tree which had drifted down and stuck in the bottom of the river so that the branches waved up and down as the current swashed through them. Jim Leonard was glad of anything that would stop the roof, and at first he thought he would get off on the tree. That was what the rat did. Perhaps the rat thought Jim Leonard really was crazy and he had better let him have the roof to himself; but the rat saw that he had made a mistake, and he jumped back again after he had swung up and down on a limb two or three times. Jim Leonard felt awfully when the rat first got into the tree, for he remembered how it said in the Pirate Book that rats always leave a sinking ship, and now he believed that he certainly was gone. But that only made him hollo the louder, and he holloed so loud that at last he made somebody hear.

It was Hen Billard's grandmother, and she put her head out of the window with her nightcap on, to see what the matter was. Jim Leonard caught sight of her, and he screamed: "Fire, fire, fire! I'm drownding, Mrs. Billard! Oh, do somebody come!" [Pg 33]

Hen Billard's grandmother just gave one yell of "Fire! The world's a-burnin' up, Hen Billard, and you layin' there sleepin' and not helpin' a bit! Somebody's out there in the river!" and she rushed into the room where Hen was, and shook him.

He bounced out of bed and pulled on his pantaloons, and was down-stairs in a minute. He ran bareheaded over to the bank, and when Jim Leonard saw him coming he holloed ten times as loud: "It's me, Hen! It's Jim Leonard! Oh, do get somebody to come out and save me! Fire!"

As soon as Hen heard that, and felt sure it was not a dream, which he did in about half a second, he began to yell, too, and to say: "How did you get there? Fire, fire, fire! What are you on? Fire! Are you in a tree, or what? Fire, fire! Are you in a flat-boat? Fire, fire, fire! If I had a skiff—fire!"

He kept racing up and down the bank, and back and forth between the bank and the houses. The river was almost up to the top of the bank, and it looked a mile wide. Down at the bridge you could hardly see any light between the water and the bridge.

Pretty soon people began to look out of their doors and windows, and Hen Billard's grandmother kept screaming: "The world's a-burnin' [Pg 34] up! The river's on fire!" Then boys came out of their houses; and then men with no hats on; and then women and girls, with their hair half down. The fire-bells began to ring, and in less than five minutes both the fire companies were on the shore, with the men at the brakes and the foremen of the companies holloing through their trumpets.

Then Jim Leonard saw what a good thing it was that he had thought of holloing fire. He felt sure now that they would save him somehow, and he made up his mind to save the rat, too, and pet it, and maybe go around and exhibit it. He would name it Bolivar; it was just the color of the elephant Bolivar that came to the Boy's Town every year. These things whirled through his brain while he watched two men setting out in a skiff toward him.

They started from the shore a little above him, and they meant to row slanting across to his tree, but the current, when they got fairly into it, swept them far below, and they were glad to row back to land again without ever getting anywhere near him. At the same time, the tree-top where his roof was caught was pulled southward by a sudden rush of the torrent; it opened, and the roof slipped out, with Jim Leonard and the rat on it. They both joined in one squeal of despair as the river leaped forward with them, [Pg 35] and a dreadful "Oh!" went up from the people on the bank.

Some of the firemen had run down to the bridge when they saw that the skiff was not going to be of any use, and one of them had got out of the window of the bridge onto the middle pier, with a long pole in his hand. It had an iron hook at the end, and it was the kind of pole that the men used to catch driftwood with and drag it ashore. When the people saw Blue Bob with that pole in his hand, they understood what he was up to. He was going to wait till the water brought the roof with Jim Leonard on it down to the bridge, and then catch the hook into the shingles and pull it up to the pier. The strongest current set close in around the middle pier, and the roof would have to pass on one side or the other. That was what Blue Bob argued out in his mind when he decided that the skiff would never reach Jim Leonard, and he knew that if he could not save him that way, nothing could save him.

Blue Bob must have had a last name, but none of the little fellows knew what it was. Everybody called him Blue Bob because he had such a thick, black beard that when he was just shaved his face looked perfectly blue. He knew all about the river and its ways, and if it had been of any use to go out with a boat, he would have gone. That was what all the boys said, when they followed [Pg 36] Blue Bob to the bridge and saw him getting out on the pier. He was the only person that the watchman had let go on the bridge for two days.

The water was up within three feet of the floor, and if Jim Leonard's roof slipped by Blue Bob's guard and passed under the bridge, it would scrape Jim Leonard off, and that would be the last of him.

All the time the roof was coming nearer the bridge, sometimes slower, sometimes faster, just as it got into an eddy or into the current; once it seemed almost to stop, and swayed completely round; then it just darted forward.

Blue Bob stood on the very point of the pier, where the strong stone-work divided the current, and held his hooked pole ready to make a clutch at the roof, whichever side it took. Jim Leonard saw him there, but although he had been holloing and yelling and crying all the time, now he was still. He wanted to say, "O Bob, save me!" but he could not make a sound.

It seemed to him that Bob was going to miss him when he made a lunge at the roof on the right side of the pier; it seemed to him that the roof was going down the left side; but he felt it quiver and stop, and then it gave a loud crack and went to pieces, and flung itself away upon the whirling and dancing flood. At first Jim Leonard thought he had gone with it; but it was only the rat that [Pg 37] tried to run up Blue Bob's pole, and slipped off into the water; and then somehow Jim was hanging onto Blue Bob's hands and scrambling onto the bridge.

Blue Bob always said he never saw any rat, and a good many people said there never was any rat on the roof with Jim Leonard; they said that he just made the rat up.

He did not mention the rat himself for several days; he told Pony Baker that he did not think of it at first, he was so excited.

Pony asked his father what he thought, and Pony's father said that it might have been the kind of rat that people see when they have been drinking too much, and that Blue Bob had not seen it because he had signed the temperance pledge.

But this was a good while after. At the time the people saw Jim Leonard standing safe with Blue Bob on the pier, they set up a regular election cheer, and they would have believed anything Jim Leonard said. They all agreed that Blue Bob had a right to go home with Jim and take him to his mother, for he had saved Jim's life, and he ought to have the credit of it.

Before this, and while everybody supposed that Jim Leonard would surely be drowned, some of the people had gone up to his mother's cabin to prepare her for the worst. She did not seem to [Pg 38] understand exactly, and she kept round getting breakfast, with her old clay pipe in her mouth; but when she got it through her head, she made an awful face, and dropped her pipe on the door-stone and broke it; and then she threw her check apron over her head and sat down and cried.

But it took so long for her to come to this that the people had not got over comforting her and trying to make her believe that it was all for the best, when Blue Bob came up through the bars with his hand on Jim's shoulder, and about all the boys in town tagging after them.

Jim's mother heard the hurrahing and pulled off her apron, and saw that Jim was safe and sound there before her. She gave him a look that made him slip round behind Blue Bob, and she went in and got a table-knife, and she came out and went to the pear-tree and cut a sucker.

She said, "I'll learn that limb to sleep in a cow-barn when he's got a decent bed in the house!" and then she started to come toward Jim Leonard.

[Pg 39]

II

LIFE IN A BOY'S TOWN

[Pg 41]

THE TOWN

I call it a Boy's Town because I wish it to appear to the reader as a town appears to a boy from his third to his eleventh year, when he seldom, if ever, catches a glimpse of life much higher than the middle of a man, and has the most distorted and mistaken views of most things.... Some people remain in this condition as long as they live, and keep the ignorance of childhood, after they have lost its innocence; heaven has been shut, but the earth is still a prison to them. These will not know what I mean by much that I shall have to say; but I hope that the ungrown-up children will, and that the boys of to-day will like to know what a boy of forty years ago was like, even if he had no very exciting adventures or thread-bare escapes; perhaps I mean hair-breadth escapes; but it is the same thing—they have been used so often. I shall try to describe him very minutely in his daily doings and dreamings, and it may amuse [Pg 42] them to compare these doings and dreamings with their own. For convenience, I shall call this boy, my boy; but I hope he might have been almost anybody's boy; and I mean him sometimes for a boy in general, as well as a boy in particular.

[Pg 43]

THE FIRST LOCK

It seems to me that my Boy's Town was a town peculiarly adapted for a boy to be a boy in. It had a river, the great Miami River, which was as blue as the sky when it was not as yellow as gold; and it had another river, called the Old River, which was the Miami's former channel, and which held an island in its sluggish loop; the boys called it The Island; and it must have been about the size of Australia; perhaps it was not so large. Then this town had a Canal, and a Canal-Basin, and a First Lock and a Second Lock; you could walk out to the First Lock, but the Second Lock was at the edge of the known world, and, when my boy was very little, the biggest boy had never been beyond it. Then it had a Hydraulic, which brought the waters of Old River for mill-power through the heart of the town, from a Big Reservoir and a Little Reservoir; the Big Reservoir was as far off as the Second Lock, and the Hydraulic ran under mysterious culverts at every street-crossing. All these streams and courses had fish in them at all seasons, and all summer long they [Pg 45] had boys in them, and now and then a boy in winter, when the thin ice of the mild Southern Ohio winter let him through with his skates. Then there were the Commons: a wide expanse of open fields, where the cows were pastured, and the boys flew their kites, and ran races, and practised for their circuses in the tan-bark rings of the real circuses.

EARLIEST MEMORIES

Some of my boy's memories reach a time earlier than his third year, and relate to the little Ohio River hamlet where he was born, and where his mother's people, who were river-faring folk, all lived. Every two or three years the river rose and flooded the village; and his grandmother's household was taken out of the second-story window in a skiff; but no one minded a trivial inconvenience like that, any more than the Romans have minded the annual freshet of the Tiber for the last three or four thousand years. When the waters went down the family returned and scrubbed out the five or six inches of rich mud they had left. In the mean time it was a godsend to all boys of an age to enjoy it; but it was nothing out of the order of Providence. So, if my boy ever saw a freshet, it naturally made no impression [Pg 46] upon him. What he remembered was something much more important, and that was waking up one morning and seeing a peach-tree in bloom through the window beside his bed; and he was always glad that this vision of beauty was his very earliest memory. All his life he has never seen a peach-tree in bloom without a swelling of the heart, without some fleeting sense that

> "Heaven lies about us in our infancy."

Over the spot where the little house once stood a railroad has drawn its erasing lines, and the house itself was long since taken down and built up brick by brick in quite another place; but the blooming peach-tree glows before his childish eyes untouched by time or change. The tender, pathetic pink of its flowers repeated itself many long years afterward in the paler tints of the almond blossoms in Italy, but always with a reminiscence of that dim past, and the little coal-smoky town on the banks of the Ohio.

Perversely blended with that vision of the blooming peach is a glimpse of a pet deer in the kitchen of the same little house, with its head up and its antlers erect, as if he meditated offence. My boy might never have seen him so; he may have had [Pg 47] the vision at second hand; but it is certain that there was a pet deer in the family, and that he was as likely to have come into the kitchen by the window as by the door. One of the boy's uncles had seen this deer swimming the Mississippi, far to the southward, and had sent out a yawl and captured him, and brought him home. He began a checkered career of uselessness when they were ferrying him over from Wheeling in a skiff, by trying to help wear the pantaloons of the boy who was holding him; he put one of his fore-legs in at the watch-pocket; but it was disagreeable to the boy and ruinous to the trousers. He grew very tame, and butted children over, right and left, in the village streets; and he behaved like one of the family whenever he got into a house; he ate the sugar out of the bowl on the table, and plundered the pantry of its sweet cakes. One day a dog got after him, and he jumped over the river-bank and broke his leg, and had to be shot.

HOME LIFE

The house gave even to him a sense of space unknown before, and he could recall his mother's satisfaction in it. He has often been back there in dreams, and found it on the old scale of grandeur; but no doubt it was a very simple affair. The [Pg 48] fortunes of a Whig editor in a place so overwhelmingly Democratic as the Boy's Town were not such as could have warranted his living in a palace; and he must have been poor, as the world goes now. But the family always lived in abundance, and in their way they belonged to the employing class; that is, the father had men to work for him. On the other hand, he worked with them; and the boys, as they grew old enough, were taught to work with them, too. My boy grew old enough very young; and was put to use in the printing-office before he was ten years of age. This was not altogether because he was needed there, I dare say, but because it was part of his father's Swedenborgian philosophy that every one should fulfil a use; I do not know that when the boy wanted to go swimming, or hunting, or skating, it consoled him much to reflect that the angels in the highest heaven delighted in uses; nevertheless, it was good for him to be of use, though maybe not so much use.

If his mother did her own work, with help only now and then from a hired girl, that was the custom of the time and country; and her memory was always the more reverend to him, because whenever he looked back at her in those dim years, he saw her about some of those household offices which are so beautiful to a child. She was always the best and tenderest mother, and [Pg 49] her love had the heavenly art of making each child feel itself the most important, while she was partial to none. In spite of her busy days she followed their father in his religion and literature, and at night, when her long toil was over, she sat with the children and listened while he read aloud.

The first book my boy remembered to have heard him read was Moore's *Lalla Rookh*, of which he formed but a vague notion, though while he struggled after its meaning he took all its music in, and began at once to make rhymes of his own. He had no conception of literature except the pleasure there was in making it; and he had no outlook into the world of it, which must have been pretty open to his father. The father read aloud some of Dickens' Christmas stories, then new; and the boy had a good deal of trouble with the *Haunted Man*. One rarest night of all, the family sat up till two o'clock, listening to a novel that my boy long ago forgot the name of, if he ever knew its name. It was all about a will, forged or lost, and there was a great scene in court, and after that the mother declared that she could not go to bed till she heard the end. His own first reading was in history. At nine years of age he read the history of Greece, and the history of Rome, and he knew that Goldsmith wrote them. One night his father told the boys all about Don Quixote; [Pg 50] and a little while after he gave my boy the book. He read it over and over again; but he did not suppose it was a novel. It was his elder brother who read novels, and a novel was like *Handy Andy*, or *Harry Lorrequer*, or the *Bride of Lammermoor*. His brother had another novel which they preferred to either; it was in Harper's old "Library of

Select Novels," and was called *Alamance; or, the Great and Final Experiment*, and it was about the life of some sort of community in North Carolina. It bewitched them, and though my boy could not afterward recall a single fact or figure in it, he could bring before his mind's eye every trait of its outward aspect.

All this went along with great and continued political excitement, and with some glimpses of the social problem. It was very simple then; nobody was very rich, and nobody was in want; but somehow, as the boy grew older, he began to discover that there were differences, even in the little world about him; some were higher and some were lower. From the first he was taught by precept and example to take the side of the lower. As the children were denied oftener than they were indulged, the margin of their own abundance must have been narrower than they ever knew then; but if they had been of the most prosperous, their bent in this matter would have been the same. Once there was a [Pg 51] church festival, or something of that sort, and there was a good deal of the provision left over, which it was decided should be given to the poor. This was very easy, but it was not so easy to find the poor whom it should be given to. At last a hard-working widow was chosen to receive it; the ladies carried it to her front door and gave it her, and she carried it to her back door and threw it into the alley. No doubt she had enough without it, but there were circumstances of indignity or patronage attending the gift which were recognized in my boy's home, and which helped afterward to make him doubtful of all giving, except the humblest, and restive with a world in which there need be any giving at all.

THE RIVER

It seems to me that the best way to get at the heart of any boy's town is to take its different watercourses and follow them into it.

The house where my boy first lived was not far from the river, and he must have seen it often before he noticed it. But he was not aware of it till he found it under the bridge. Without the river there could not have been a bridge; the fact of the bridge may have made him look for the river; but the bridge is foremost in his mind. [Pg 52] It is a long, wooden tunnel, with two roadways, and a foot-path on either side of these; there is a toll-house at each end, and from one to the other it is about as far as from the Earth to the planet Mars. On the western shore of the river is a smaller town than the Boy's Town, and in the perspective the entrance of the bridge on that side is like a dim little doorway. The timbers are of a hugeness to strike fear into the heart of the boldest little boy; and there is something awful even about the dust in the roadways; soft and thrillingly cool to the boy's bare feet, it lies thick in a perpetual twilight, streaked at intervals by the sun that slants in at the high, narrow windows under the roof; it has a certain potent, musty smell. The bridge has three piers, and at low water hardier adventurers than he wade out to the middle pier; some heroes even fish there, standing all day on the loose rocks about the base of the pier. He shudders to see them, and aches with wonder how they will get ashore. Once he is there when a big boy wades back from the middle pier, where he has been to rob a goose's nest; he has some loose silver change in his wet hand, and my boy understands that it has come out of one of the goose eggs. This fact, which he never thought of questioning, gets mixed up in his mind with an idea of riches, of treasure-trove, in the cellar of an old house [Pg 53] that has been torn down near the end of the bridge.

The river had its own climate, and this climate was of course much such a climate as the boys, for whom nature intended the river, would have chosen. I do not believe it was ever winter there, though it was sometimes late autumn, so that the boys could have some use for the caves they dug at the top of the bank, with a hole coming through the turf, to let out the smoke of the fires they built inside. They had the joy of choking and blackening over these flues, and they intended to live on corn and potatoes borrowed from the household stores of the boy whose house was nearest. They never got so far as to parch the corn or to bake the potatoes in their caves, but there was the fire, and the draught was magnificent. The light of the red flames painted the little, happy, foolish faces, so long since wrinkled and grizzled with age, or mouldered away to dust, as the boys huddled before them under the bank, and fed them with the drift, or stood patient of the heat and cold in the afternoon light of some vast Saturday waning to nightfall.

The river-climate, with these autumnal intervals, was made up of a quick, eventful springtime, followed by the calm of a cloudless summer that seemed never to end. But the spring, short as it was, had its great attractions, and chief of these [Pg 54] was the freshet which it brought to the river. They would hear somehow that the river was rising, and then the boys, who had never connected its rise with the rains they must have been having, would all go down to its banks and watch the swelling waters. These would be yellow and thick, and the boiling current would have smooth, oily eddies, where pieces of drift would whirl round and round, and then escape and slip down the stream. There were saw-logs and whole trees with their branching tops, lengths of fence and hen-coops and pig-pens; once there was a stable; and if the flood continued, there began to come swollen bodies of horses and cattle. This must have meant serious loss to the people living on the river-bottoms above, but the boys counted it all gain. They cheered the objects as they floated by, and they were breathless with the excitement of seeing the men who caught fence-rails and cord-wood, and even saw-logs, with iron prongs at the points of long poles, as they stood on some jutting point of shore and stretched far out over the flood. The boys exulted in the turbid spread of the stream, which filled its low western banks and stole over their tops, and washed into all the hollow places along its shores, and shone among the trunks of the sycamores on Delorac's Island, which was almost of the geographical importance of The Island in Old River. When the water [Pg 55] began to go down their hearts sank with it; and they gave up the hope of seeing the bridge carried away. Once the river rose to within a few feet of it, so that if the right piece of drift had been there to do its duty, the bridge might have been torn from its piers and swept down the raging tide into those unknown gulfs to the southward. Many a time they went to bed full of hope that it would at least happen in the night, and woke to learn with shame and grief in the morning that the bridge was still there, and the river was falling. It was a little comfort to know that some of the big boys had almost seen it go, watching as far into the night as nine o'clock with the men who sat up near the bridge till daylight: men of leisure and public spirit, but not perhaps the leading citizens.

SWIMMING

There must have been a tedious time between the going down of the flood and the first days when the water was warm enough for swimming; but it left no trace. The boys are standing on the shore while the freshet rushes by, and then they are in the water, splashing, diving, ducking; it is like that; so that I do not know just how to get in that period of fishing which must always have come between. There were not many fish in that [Pg 56] part of the Miami; my boy's experience was full of the ignominy of catching shiners and suckers, or, at the best, mudcats, as they called the yellow catfish; but there were boys, of those who cursed and swore, who caught sunfish, as they called the bream; and there were men who were reputed to catch at will, as it were, silvercats and river-bass. They fished with minnows, which they kept in battered tin buckets that they did not allow you even to touch, or hardly to look at; my boy scarcely breathed in their presence; when one of them got up to cast his line in a new place, the boys all ran, and then came slowly back. These men often carried a flask of liquid that had the property, when taken inwardly, of keeping the damp out. The boys respected them for their ability to drink whiskey, and thought it a fit and honorable thing that they should now and then fall into the river over the brinks where they had set their poles. But they disappear like persons in a dream, and their fishing-time vanishes with them, and the swimming-time is in full possession of the river, and of all the other waters of the Boy's Town. [Pg 57]

The swimming-holes in the river were the greatest favorites. My boy could not remember when he began to go into them, though it certainly was before he could swim. There was a time when he was afraid of getting in over his head; but he did not know just when he learned to swim, any more than he knew when he learned to read; he could not swim, and then he could swim; he could not read, and then he could read; but I dare say the reading came somewhat before the swimming. Yet the swimming must have come very early, and certainly it was kept up with continual practise; he swam quite as much as he read; perhaps more. The boys had deep swimming-holes and shallow ones; and over the deep ones there was always a spring-board, from which they threw somersaults, or dived straight down into the depths, where there were warm and cold currents mysteriously interwoven. They believed that these deep holes were infested by water-snakes, though they never saw any, and they expected to be bitten by snapping-turtles, though this never happened. Fiery dragons could not have kept them out; gallynippers, whatever they were, certainly did not; they were believed to abound at the bottom of the deep holes; but the boys never stayed long in the deep holes, and they preferred the shallow places, where the river broke into a long ripple (they called it riffle) on [Pg 58] its gravelly bed, and where they could at once soak and bask in the musical rush of the sunlit waters. I have heard people in New England blame all the Western rivers for being yellow and turbid; but I know that after the spring floods, when the Miami had settled down to its summer business with the boys, it was as clear and as blue as if it were spilled out of the summer sky. The boys liked the riffle because they could stay in so long there, and there were little land-locked pools and shallows, where the water was even warmer, and they could stay in longer. At most places under the banks there was clay of different colors, which they used for war-paint in their Indian fights; and after they had their Indian fights they could rush screaming and clattering into the riffle. When the stream had washed them clean down to their red sunburn or their leathern tan, they could paint up again and have more Indian fights.

I wonder what sign the boys who read this have for challenging or inviting one another to go in swimming. The boys in the Boy's Town used to make the motion of swimming with both arms; or they held up the forefinger and middle-finger in the form of a swallow-tail; they did this when it was necessary to be secret about it, as in school, and when they did not want the whole crowd of boys to come along; and often when they just pretended they did not want some [Pg 59] one to know. They really had to be secret at times, for some of the boys were not allowed to go in at all; others were forbidden to go in more than once or twice a day; and as they all *had* to go in at least three or four times a day, some sort of sign had to be used that was understood among themselves alone. Since this is a true history, I had better own that they nearly all, at one time or other, must have told lies about it, either before or after the fact, some habitually, some only in great extremity. Here and there a boy, like my boy's elder brother, would not tell lies at all, even about going in swimming; but by far the greater number bowed to their hard fate, and told them. They promised that they would not go in, and then they said that they had not been in; but Sin, for which they had made this sacrifice, was apt to betray them. Either they got their shirts on wrong side out in dressing, or else, while they were in, some enemy came upon them and tied their shirts. There are few cruelties which public opinion in the boy's world condemns, but I am glad to remember, to their honor, that there were not many in that Boy's Town who would tie shirts; and I fervently hope that there is no boy now living who would do it. As the crime is probably extinct, I will say that in those wicked days, if you were such a miscreant, and there was some boy you hated, [Pg 60] you stole up and tied the hardest kind of a knot in one arm or both arms of his shirt. Then, if the Evil One put it into your heart, you soaked the knot in water, and pounded it with a stone.

I am glad to know that in the days when he was thoughtless and senseless enough, my boy never was guilty of any degree of this meanness. It was his brother, I suppose, who taught him to abhor it; and perhaps it was his own suffering from it in part; for he, too, sometimes shed bitter tears over such a knot, as I have seen hapless little wretches do, tearing at it with their nails and gnawing at it with their teeth, knowing that the time was passing when they could hope to hide the fact that they had been in swimming, and foreseeing no remedy but to cut off the sleeve above the knot, or else put on their clothes without the shirt, and trust to untying the knot when it got dry.

There must have been a lurking anxiety in all the boys' hearts when they went in without leave, or, as my boy was apt to do, when explicitly forbidden. He was not apt at lying, I dare say, and so he took the course of open disobedience. He could not see the danger that filled the home hearts with fear for him, and he must have often broken the law and been forgiven, before Justice one day appeared for him on the river-bank and called him away from his stolen joys. It was [Pg 61] an awful moment, and it covered him with shame before his mates, who heartlessly rejoiced, as children do, in the doom which they are escaping. That sin, at least, he fully expiated; and I will whisper to the young people here at the end of the chapter that somehow, soon or late, our sins do overtake us, and insist upon being paid for. That is not the best reason for not sinning, but it is well to know it, and to believe it in our acts as well as our thoughts. You will find people to tell you that things only happen so and so. It may be; only, I know that no good thing ever happened to happen to me when I had done wrong.

SKATING

I am afraid that the young people will think I am telling them too much about swimming. But in the Boy's Town the boys really led a kind of amphibious life, and as long as the long summer lasted they were almost as much in the water as on the land. The Basin, however, unlike the river, had a winter as well as a summer climate, and one of the very first things that my boy could remember was being on the ice there. He learned to skate, but he did not know when, any more than he knew just the moment of learning to read or to swim. He became passionately fond of [Pg 62] skating, and kept at it all day long when there was ice for it, which was not often in those soft winters. They made a very little ice go a long way in the Boy's Town; and began to use it for skating as soon as there was a glazing of it on the Basin. None of them ever got drowned there; though a boy would often start from one bank and go flying to the other, trusting his speed to save him, while the thin sheet sank and swayed, but never actually broke under him. Usually the ice was not thick enough to have a fire built on it; and it must have been on ice which was just strong enough to bear that my boy skated all one bitter afternoon at Old River, without a fire to warm by. At first his feet were very cold, and then they gradually felt less cold, and at last he did not feel them at all. He thought this very nice, and he told one of the big boys. "Why, your feet are frozen!" said the big boy, and he dragged off my boy's skates, and the little one ran all the long mile home, crazed with terror, and not knowing what moment his feet might drop off there in the road. His mother plunged them in a bowl of ice-cold water, and then rubbed them with flannel, and so thawed them out; but that could not save him from the pain of their coming to: it was intense, and there must have been a time afterward when he did not use his feet. [Pg 63]

His skates themselves were of a sort that I am afraid boys would smile at nowadays. When you went to get a pair of skates forty or fifty years ago, you did not make your choice between a Barney & Berry and an Acme, which fastened on with the turn of a screw or the twist of a clamp. You found an assortment of big and little sizes of solid wood bodies with guttered blades turning up in front with a sharp point, or perhaps curling over above the toe. In this case they sometimes ended in an acorn; if this acorn was of brass, it transfigured the boy who wore that skate; he might have been otherwise all rags and patches, but the brass acorn made him splendid from head to foot. When you had bought your skates, you took them to a carpenter, and stood awe-strickenly about while he pierced the wood with strap-holes; or else you managed to bore them through with a hot iron yourself. Then you took them to a saddler, and got him to make straps for them; that is, if you were rich, and your father let you have a quarter to pay for the job. If not, you put strings through, and tied your skates on. They were always coming off, or getting crosswise of your foot, or feeble-mindedly slumping down on one side of the wood; but it did not matter, if you had a fire on the ice, fed with old barrels and boards and cooper's shavings, and could sit round it with [Pg 64] your skates on, and talk and tell stones, between your flights and races afar; and come whizzing back to it from the frozen distance, and glide, with one foot lifted, almost among the embers.

MANNERS AND CUSTOMS

I sometimes wonder how much these have changed since my boy's time. Of course they differ somewhat from generation to generation, and from East to West and North to South, but not so much, I believe, as grown people are apt to think. Everywhere and always the world of boys is outside of the laws that govern grown-up communities, and it has its unwritten usages, which are handed down from old to young, and perpetuated on the same level of years, and are lived into and lived out of, but are binding, through all personal vicissitudes, upon the great body of boys between six and twelve years old. No boy can violate them without losing his standing among the other boys, and he cannot enter into their world without coming under them. He must do this, and must not do that;

he obeys, but he does not know why, any more than the far-off savages from whom his customs seem mostly to have come. His world is all in and through the world of men and women, but no [Pg 65] man or woman can get into it any more than if it were a world of invisible beings. It has its own ideals and superstitions, and these are often of a ferocity, a depravity, scarcely credible in after-life. It is a great pity that fathers and mothers cannot penetrate that world; but they cannot, and it is only by accident that they can catch some glimpse of what goes on in it. No doubt it will be civilized in time, but it will be very slowly; and in the mean while it is only in some of its milder manners and customs that the boy's world can be studied.

The first great law was that, whatever happened to you through another boy, whatever hurt or harm he did you, you were to right yourself upon his person if you could; but if he was too big, and you could not hope to revenge yourself, then you were to bear the wrong, not only for that time, but for as many times as he chose to inflict it. To tell the teacher or your mother, or to betray your tormentor to any one outside of the boys' world, was to prove yourself a cry-baby, without honor or self-respect, and unfit to go with the other fellows. They would have the right to mock you, to point at you, and call "E-e-e, e-e-e, e-e-e!" at you, till you fought them. After that, whether you whipped them or not, there began to be some feeling in your favor again, and they had to stop. [Pg 66]

Every boy who came to town from somewhere else, or who moved into a new neighborhood, had to fight the old residents. There was no reason for this, except that he was a stranger, and there appeared to be no other means of making his acquaintance. If he was generally whipped he became subject to the local tribe, as the Delawares were to the Iroquois in the last century; if he whipped the other boys, then they adopted him into their tribe, and he became a leader among them. When you moved away from a neighborhood you did not lose all your rights in it; you did not have to fight when you went back to see the boys, or anything; but if one of them met you in your new precincts you might have to try conclusions with him; and perhaps, if he was a boy who had been in the habit of whipping you, you were quite ready to do so. When my boy's family left the Smith house, one of the boys from that neighborhood came up to see him at the Falconer house, and tried to carry things with a high hand, as he always had done. Then my boy fought him, quite as if he were not a Delaware and the other boy not an Iroquois, with sovereign rights over him. My boy was beaten, but the difference was that, if he had not been on new ground, he would have been beaten without daring to fight. His mother witnessed the combat, and came out and shamed him for his behavior, [Pg 67] and had in the other boy, and made them friends over some sugar-cakes. But after that the boys of the Smith neighborhood understood that my boy would not be whipped without fighting. The home instruction was all against fighting; my boy was taught that it was not only wicked but foolish; that if it was wrong to strike, it was just as wrong to strike back; that two wrongs never made a right, and so on. But all this was not of the least effect with a hot temper amid the trials and perplexities of life in the Boy's Town.

Their fights were mostly informal scuffles, on and off in a flash, and conducted with none of the ceremony which I have read of concerning the fights of English boys. It was believed that some of the fellows knew how to box, and all the fellows intended to learn, but nobody ever did. The fights sprang usually out of some trouble of the moment; but at times they were arranged to settle some question of moral or physical superiority. Then one boy put a chip on his shoulder and dared the other to knock it off. It took a great while to bring the champions to blows, and I have known the mere preparatory insults of a fight of this kind to wear out the spirit of the combatants and the patience of the spectators, so that not a blow was struck, finally, and the whole affair fell through. [Pg 68]

GIRLS

Though they were so quarrelsome among themselves, the boys that my boy went with never molested girls. They mostly ignored them; but they would have scorned to hurt a girl almost as much as they would have scorned to play with one. Of course, while they were very little, they played with girls; and after they began to be big boys, eleven or twelve years old, they began to pay girls some attention; but for the rest they simply left them out of the question, except at parties, when the games obliged them to take some notice of the girls. Even then, however, it was not good form for a boy to be greatly interested in them; and he had to conceal any little fancy he had about this girl or that unless he wanted to be considered soft by the other fellows. When they were having fun they did not want to have any girls around; but in the back-yard a boy might play teeter or seesaw, or some such thing, with his sisters and their friends, without necessarily losing caste, though such things were not encouraged. On the other hand, a boy was bound to defend them against anything that he thought slighting or insulting; and you did not have to verify the fact that anything had been said or done; you merely had to hear that it had. [Pg 69]

MOTHERS

The boys had very little to do with the inside of one another's houses. They would follow a boy to his door, and wait for him to come out; and they would sometimes get him to go in and ask his mother for crullers or sugar-cakes; when they came to see him they never went indoors for him, but stood on the sidewalk and called him with a peculiar cry, something like "E-oo-we, e-oo-we!" and threw stones at trees, or anything, till he came out. If he did not come after a reasonable time, they knew he was not there, or that his mother would not let him come. A fellow was kept in that way, now and then. If a fellow's mother came to the door the boys always ran.

The mother represented the family sovereignty; the father was seldom seen, and he counted for little or nothing among the outside boys. It was the mother who could say whether a boy might go fishing or in swimming, and she was held a good mother or not according as she habitually said yes or no. There was no other standard of goodness for mothers in the boy's world, and could be none; and a bad mother might be outwitted by any device that the other boys could suggest to her boy. Such a boy was always willing [Pg 70] to listen to any suggestion, and no boy took it hard if the other fellows made fun when their plan got him into trouble at home. If a boy came out after some such experience with his face wet, and his eyes red, and his lips swollen, of course you had to laugh; he expected it, and you expected him to stone you for laughing.

When a boy's mother had company, he went and hid till the guests were gone, or only came out of concealment to get some sort of shy lunch. If the other fellows' mothers were there, he might be a little bolder, and bring out cake from the second table. But he had to be pretty careful how he conformed to any of the usages of grown-up society. A fellow who brushed his hair, and put on shoes, and came into the parlor when there was company, was not well seen among the fellows; he was regarded in some degree as a girl-boy; a boy who wished to stand well with other boys kept in the wood-shed, and only went in as far as the kitchen to get things for his guests in the back-yard. Yet there were mothers who would make a boy put on a collar when they had company, and disgrace him before the world by making him stay round and help; they acted as if they had no sense and no pity; but such mothers were rare.

Most mothers yielded to public opinion and let their boys leave the house, and wear just what [Pg 71] they always wore. I have told how little they wore in summer. Of course in winter they had to put on more things. In those days knickerbockers were unknown, and if a boy had appeared in short pants and long stockings he would have been thought dressed like a circus-actor. Boys wore long pantaloons, like men, as soon as they put off skirts, and they wore jackets or roundabouts such as the English boys still wear at Eton. When the cold weather came they had to put on shoes and stockings, or rather long-legged boots, such as are seen now only among lumbermen and teamsters in the country. Most of the fellows had stoga boots, as heavy as iron and as hard; they were splendid to skate in, they kept your ankles so stiff. Sometimes they greased them to keep the water out; but they never blacked them except on Sunday, and before Saturday they were as red as a rusty stovepipe. At night they were always so wet that you could not get them off without a boot-jack, and you could hardly do it anyway; sometimes you got your brother to help you off with them, and then he pulled you all round the room. In the morning they were dry, but just as hard as stone, and you had to soap the heel of your woollen sock (which your grandmother had knitted for you, or maybe some of your aunts) before you could get your foot in, and sometimes the ears of [Pg 72] the boot that you pulled it on by would give way, and you would have to stamp your foot in and kick the toe against the mop-board. Then you gasped and limped round, with your feet like fire, till you could get out and limber your boots up in some water somewhere. About noon your chilblains began.

I have tried to give some notion of the general distribution of comfort, which was never riches, in the Boy's Town; but I am afraid that I could not paint the simplicity of things there truly without being misunderstood in these days of great splendor and great squalor. Everybody had enough, but nobody had too much; the richest man in town might be worth twenty thousand dollars. There were distinctions among the grown people, and no doubt there were the social cruelties which are the modern expression of the savage spirit otherwise repressed by civilization; but these were unknown among the boys. Savages they were, but not that kind of savages. They valued a boy for his character and prowess, and it did not matter in the least that he was ragged and dirty. Their mothers might not allow him the run of their kitchens quite so freely as some other boys, but the boys went with him just the same, and they never noticed how little he was washed and dressed. The best of them had not an overcoat; and underclothing was unknown [Pg 73] among them. When a boy had buttoned up his roundabout, and put on his mittens, and tied his comforter round his neck and over his ears, he was warmly dressed.

A BROTHER

My boy was often kept from being a fool, and worse, by that elder brother of his; and I advise every boy to have an elder brother. Have a brother about four years older than yourself, I should say; and if your temper is hot, and your disposition revengeful, and you are a vain and ridiculous dreamer at the same time that you are eager to excel in feats of strength and games of skill, and to do everything that the other fellows do, and are ashamed to be better than the worst boy in the crowd, your brother can be of the greatest use to you, with his larger experience and wisdom. My boy's brother seemed to have an ideal of usefulness, while my boy only had an ideal of glory—to wish to help others, while my boy only wished to help himself. My boy would as soon have thought of his father's doing a wrong thing as of his brother's doing it; and his brother was a calm light of common-sense, of justice, of truth, while he was a fantastic flicker of gaudy purposes which he wished to make shine before men in [Pg 74] their fulfilment. His brother was always doing for him and for the younger children; while my boy only did for himself; he had a very gray mustache before he began to have any conception of the fact that he was sent into the world to serve and to suffer, as well as to rule and enjoy. But his brother seemed to know this instinctively; he bore the yoke in his youth, patiently if not willingly; he shared the anxieties as he parted the cares of his father and mother. Yet he was a boy among boys, too; he loved to swim, to skate, to fish, to forage, and passionately, above all, he loved to hunt; but in everything he held himself in check, that he might hold the younger boys in check; and my boy often repaid his conscientious vigilance with hard words and hard names, such as embitter even the most self-forgiving memories. He kept mechanically within certain laws, and though in his rage he hurled every other name at his brother, he would not call him a fool, because then he would be in danger of hell-fire. If he had known just what Raca meant, he might have called him Raca, for he was not so much afraid of the council; but, as it was, his brother escaped that insult, and held through all a rein upon him, and governed him through his scruples as well as his fears.

His brother was full of inventions and enterprises beyond most other boys, and his undertakings [Pg 75] came to the same end of nothingness that awaits all boyish endeavor. He intended to make fireworks and sell them; he meant to raise silkworms; he prepared to take the contract of clearing the new cemetery grounds of stumps by blasting them out with gunpowder. Besides this, he had a plan with another big boy for making money, by getting slabs from the saw-mill, and sawing them up into stove-wood, and selling them to the cooks of canal-boats. The only trouble was that the cooks would not buy the fuel, even when the boys had a half-cord of it all nicely piled up on the canal-bank; they would rather come ashore after dark and take it for nothing. He had a good many other schemes for getting rich that failed; and he wanted to go to California and dig gold; only his mother would not consent. He really did save the Canal-Basin once, when the banks began to give way after a long rain. He saw the break beginning, and ran to tell his father, who had the fire-bells rung. The fire companies came rushing to the rescue, but as they could not put the Basin out with their engines, they all got shovels and kept it in. They did not do this before it had overflowed the street, and run into the cellars of the nearest houses. The water stood two feet deep in the kitchen of my boy's house, and the yard was flooded so that the boys made rafts and navigated it for a whole day. [Pg 76] My boy's brother got drenched to the skin in the rain, and lots of fellows fell off the rafts.

He belonged to a military company of big boys that had real wooden guns, such as the little boys never could get, and silk oilcloth caps, and nankeen roundabouts, and white pantaloons with black stripes down the legs; and once they marched out to a boy's that had a father that had a farm, and he gave them all a free dinner in an arbor before the house: bread-and-butter, and apple-butter, and molasses and pound cake, and peaches and apples; it was splendid. When the excitement about the Mexican War was the highest, the company wanted a fort; and they got a farmer to come and scale off the sod with his plough, in a grassy place there was near a piece of woods, where a good many cows were pastured. They took the pieces of sod, and built them up into the walls of a fort about fifteen feet square; they intended to build them higher than their heads, but they got so eager to have the works stormed that they could not wait, and they commenced having the battle when they had the walls only breast high. There were going to be two parties: one to attack the fort, and the other to defend it, and they were just going to throw sods; but one boy had a real shot-gun, that he was to load up with powder and fire off when the battle got to the worst, so as to have it [Pg 77] more like a battle. He thought it would be more like yet if he put in a few shot, and he did it on his own hook. It was a splendid gun, but it would not stand cocked long, and he was resting it on the wall of the fort, ready to fire when the storming-party came on, throwing sods and yelling and holloing; and all at once his gun went off, and a cow that was grazing broadside to the fort gave a frightened bellow, and put up her tail, and started for home. When they found out that the gun, if not the boy, had shot a cow, the Mexicans and Americans both took to their heels; and it was a good thing they did so, for as soon as that cow got home, and the owner found out by the blood on her that she had been shot, though it was only a very slight wound, he was so mad that he did not know what to do, and very likely he would have half killed those boys if he had caught them. He got a plough, and he went out to their fort, and he ploughed it all down flat, so that not one sod remained upon another.

My boy's brother went to all sorts of places that my boy was too shy to go to; and he associated with much older boys, but there was one boy who, as I have said, was the dear friend of both of them, and that was the boy who came to learn the trade in their father's printing-office, and who began an historical romance at the time my boy began his great Moorish novel. The [Pg 78] first day he came he was put to roll, or ink, the types, while my boy's brother worked the press, and all day long my boy, from where he was setting type, could hear him telling the story of a book he had read. It was about a person named Monte Cristo, who was a count, and who could do anything. My boy listened with a gnawing literary jealousy of a boy who had read a book that he had never heard of. He tried to think whether it sounded as if it were as great a book as the *Conquest of Granada*, or *Gesta Romanorum*; and for a time he kept aloof from this boy because of his envy. Afterward they came together on *Don Quixote*, but though my boy came to have quite a passionate fondness for him, he was long in getting rid of his grudge against him for his knowledge of *Monte Cristo*. He was as great a laugher as my boy and his brother, and he liked the same sports, so that two by two, or all three together, they had no end of jokes and fun. He became the editor of a country newspaper, with varying fortunes but steadfast principles, and when the war broke out he went as a private soldier. He soon rose to be an officer, and fought bravely in many battles. Then he came back to a country-newspaper office where, ever after, he continued to fight the battles of right against wrong, till he died not long ago at his post of duty—a true, generous, and [Pg 79] lofty soul. He was one of those boys who grow into the men who seem commoner in America than elsewhere, and who succeed far beyond our millionaires and statesmen in realizing the ideal of America in their nobly simple lives. If his story could be faithfully written out, word for word, deed for deed, it would be far more thrilling than that of Monte Cristo, or any hero of romance; and so would the common story of any common life. But we cannot tell these stories, somehow.

A FRIEND

My boy's closest friend was a boy who was probably never willingly at school in his life, and who had no more relish of literature or learning in him than the open fields, or the warm air of an early spring day. I dare say it was a sense of his kinship with Nature that took my boy with him, and rested his soul from all its wild dreams and vain imaginings. He was like a piece of the genial earth, with no more hint of toiling or spinning in him; willing for anything, but passive, and without force or aim. He lived in a belated log-cabin that stood in the edge of a cornfield on the river-bank, and he seemed, one day when my boy went to find him there, to have a mother, who smoked a cob-pipe, and two or three large sisters who [Pg 80] hulked about in the one dim, low room. But the boys had very little to do with each other's houses, or, for that matter, with each other's yards. His friend seldom entered my boy's gate, and never his door; for with all the toleration his father felt for every manner of human creature, he could not see what good the boy was to get from this queer companion. It is certain that he got no harm; for his companion was too vague and void even to think evil. Socially, he was as low as the ground under foot, but morally he was as good as any boy in the Boy's Town, and he had no bad impulses. He had no impulses at all, in fact, and of his own motion he never did anything, or seemed to think anything. When he wished to get at my boy, he simply appeared in the neighborhood, and hung about the outside of the fence till he came out. He did not whistle, or call "E-oo-we!" as the other fellows did, but waited patiently to be discovered, and to be gone off with wherever my boy listed. He never had any plans himself, and never any will but to go in swimming; he neither hunted nor foraged; he did not even fish; and I suppose that money could not have hired him to run races. He played marbles, but not very well, and he did not care much for the game. The two boys soaked themselves in the river together, and then they lay on the sandy shore, or under some tree, and talked; but [Pg 81] my boy could not have talked to him about any of the things that were in his books, or the fume of dreams they sent up in his mind. He must rather have soothed against his soft, caressing ignorance the ache of his fantastic spirit, and reposed his intensity of purpose in that lax and easy aimlessness. Their friendship was not only more innocent than any other friendship my boy had, but it was wholly innocent; they loved each other, and that was all; and why people love one another there is never any satisfactory telling. But this friend of his must have had great natural good in him; and if I could find a man of the make of that boy I am sure I should love him.

My boy's other friends wondered at his fondness for him, and it was often made a question with him at home, if not a reproach to him; so that in the course of time it ceased to be that comfort it had been to him. He could not give him up, but he could not help seeing that he was ignorant and idle, and in a fatal hour he resolved to reform him. I am not able to say now just how he worked his friend up to the point of coming to school, and of washing his hands and feet and face, and putting on a new check shirt to come in. But one day he came, and my boy, as he had planned, took him into his seat, and owned his friendship with him before the whole school. This was not easy, for though everybody knew [Pg 82] how much the two were together, it was a different thing to sit with him as if he thought him just as good as any boy, and to help him get his lessons, and stay him mentally as well as socially. He struggled through one day, and maybe another; but it was a failure from the first moment, and my boy breathed freer when his friend came one half-day, and then never came again. The attempted reform had spoiled their simple and harmless intimacy. They never met again upon the old ground of perfect trust and affection. Perhaps the kindly earth-spirit had instinctively felt a wound from the shame my boy had tried to brave out, and shrank from their former friendship without quite knowing why. Perhaps it was my boy who learned to realize that there could be little in common but their common humanity between them, and could not go back to that. At any rate, their friendship declined from this point; and it seems to me, somehow, a pity.

Among the boys who were between my boy and his brother in age was one whom all the boys liked, because he was clever with everybody, with little boys as well as big boys. He was a laughing, pleasant fellow, always ready for fun, but he never did mean things, and he had an open face that made a friend of every one who saw him. He had a father that had a house with a lightning-rod, so that if you were [Pg 83] in it when there was a thunder-storm you could not get struck by lightning, as my boy once proved by being in it when there was a thunder-storm and not getting struck. This in itself was a great merit, and there were grape-arbors and peach-trees in his yard which added to his popularity, with cling-stone peaches almost as big as oranges on them. He was a fellow who could take you home to meals whenever he wanted to, and he liked to have boys stay all night with him; his mother was as clever as he was, and even the sight of his father did not make the fellows want to go and hide. His father was so clever that he went home with my boy one night about midnight when the boy had come to pass the night with his boys, and the youngest of them had said he always had the nightmare and walked in his sleep, and as likely as not he might kill you before he knew it. My boy tried to sleep, but the more he reflected upon his chances of getting through the night alive the smaller they seemed; and so he woke up his potential murderer from the sweetest and soundest slumber, and said he was going home, but he was afraid; and the boy had to go and wake his father. Very few fathers would have dressed up and gone home with a boy at midnight, and perhaps this one did so only because the mother made him; but it shows how clever the whole family was. [Pg 84]

It was their oldest boy whom my boy and his brother chiefly went with before that boy who knew about *Monte Cristo* came to learn the trade in their father's office. One Saturday in July they three spent the whole day together. It was just the time when the apples are as big as walnuts on the trees, and a boy wants to try whether any of them are going to be sweet or not. The boys tried a great many of them, in an old orchard thrown open for building-lots behind my boy's yard; but they could not find any that were not sour; or that they could eat till they thought of putting salt on them; if you put salt on it, you could eat any kind of green apple, whether it was going to be a sweet kind or not. They went up to the Basin bank and got lots of salt out of the holes in the barrels lying there, and then they ate all the apples they could hold, and after that they cut limber sticks off the trees, and sharpened the points, and stuck apples on them and threw them. You could send an apple almost out of sight that way, and you could scare a dog almost as far as you could see him.

On Monday my boy and his brother went to school, but the other boy was not there, and in the afternoon they heard he was sick. Then, toward the end of the week they heard that he had the flux; and on Friday, just before school let out, the teacher—it was the one that whipped [Pg 85] so, and that the fellows all liked—rapped on his desk, and began to speak very solemnly to the scholars. He told them that their little mate, whom they had played with and studied with, was lying very sick, so very sick that it was expected he would die; and then he read them a serious lesson about life and death, and tried to make them feel how passing and uncertain all things were, and resolve to live so that they need never be afraid to die.

Some of the fellows cried, and the next day some of them went to see the dying boy, and my boy went with them. His spirit was stricken to the earth, when he saw his gay, kind playmate lying there, white as the pillow under his wasted face, in which his sunken blue eyes showed large and strange. The sick boy did not say anything that the other boys could hear, but they could see the wan smile that came to his dry lips, and the light come sadly into his eyes, when his mother asked him if he knew this one or that; and they could not bear it, and went out of the room.

In a few days they heard that he was dead, and one afternoon school did not keep, so that the boys might go to the funeral. Most of them walked in the procession; but some of them were waiting beside the open grave, that was dug near the grave of that man who believed there was a hole through the earth from pole to pole, and had a perforated stone globe on top of his monument.

III

GAMES AND PASTIMES

[Pg 89]

MARBLES

In the Boy's Town they had regular games and plays, which came and went in a stated order. The first thing in the spring, as soon as the frost began to come out of the ground, they had marbles which they played till the weather began to be pleasant for the game, and then they left it off. There were some mean-spirited fellows who played for fun, but any boy who was anything played for keeps: that is, keeping all the marbles he won. As my boy was skilful at marbles, he was able to start out in the morning with his toy, or the marble he shot with, and a commy, or a brown marble of the lowest value, and come home at night with a pocketful of white-alleys and blood-alleys, striped plasters and bull's-eyes, and crystals, clear and clouded. His gambling was not approved of at home, but it was allowed him because of the hardness of his heart, I suppose, and because it was not thought well to keep him up too strictly; and I suspect it would have been useless to forbid his playing for keeps, though he came to have a bad conscience about it before he gave it [Pg 90] up. There were three kinds of games at marbles which the boys played: one with a long ring marked out on the ground, and a base some distance off, which you began to shoot from; another with a round ring, whose line formed the base; and another with holes, three or five, hollowed in the earth at equal distances from each other, which was called knucks. You could play for keeps in all these games; and in knucks, if you won, you had a shot or shots at the knuckles of the fellow who lost, and who was obliged to hold them down for you to shoot at. Fellows who were mean would twitch their knuckles away when they saw your toy coming, and run; but most of them took their punishment with the savage pluck of so many little Sioux. As the game began in the raw cold of the earliest spring, every boy had chapped hands, and nearly every one had the skin worn off the knuckle of his middle finger from resting it on the ground when he shot. You could use a knuckle-dabster of fur or cloth to rest your hand on, but is was considered effeminate, and in the excitement you were apt to forget it, anyway. Marbles were always very exciting, and were played with a clamor as incessant as that of a blackbird roost. A great many points were always coming up: whether a boy took-up, or edged, beyond the very place where his toy lay when he shot; whether he knuckled down, or kept his hand [Pg 91] on the ground, in shooting; whether, when another boy's toy drove one marble against another and knocked both out of the ring, he holloed "Fen doubs!" before the other fellow holloed "Doubs!" whether a marble was in or out of the ring, and whether the umpire's decision was just or not. The gambling and the quarrelling went on till the second-bell rang for school, and began again as soon as the boys could get back to their rings when school let out. The rings were usually marked on the ground with a stick, but when there was a great hurry, or there was no stick handy, the side of a fellow's boot would do, and the hollows for knucks were always bored by twirling round on your boot-heel. This helped a boy to wear out his boots very rapidly, but that was what his boots were made for, just as the sidewalks were made for the boys' marble-rings, and a citizen's character for cleverness or meanness was fixed by his walking round or over the rings. Cleverness was used in the Virginia sense for amiability; a person who was clever in the English sense was smart.

RACES

When the warm weather came on in April, and the boys got off their shoes for good, there came races, in which they seemed to fly on wings. [Pg 92] Life has a good many innocent joys for the human animal, but surely none so ecstatic as the boy feels when his bare foot first touches the breast of our mother earth in the spring. Something thrills through him then from the heart of her inmost being that makes him feel kin with her, and cousin to all her dumb children of the grass and trees. His blood leaps as wildly as at that kiss of the waters when he plunges into their arms in June; there is something even finer and sweeter in the rapture of the earlier bliss. The day will not be long enough for his flights, his races; he aches more with regret than with fatigue when he must leave the happy paths under the stars outside, and creep into his bed. It is all like some glimpse, some foretaste of the heavenly time when the earth and her sons shall be reconciled in a deathless love, and they shall not be thankless, nor she a stepmother any more.

About the only drawback to going barefoot was stumping your toe, which you were pretty sure to do when you first took off your shoes and before you had got used to your new running weight. [Pg 93] When you struck your toe against a rock, or anything, you caught it up in your hand, and hopped about a hundred yards before you could bear to put it to the ground. Then you sat down, and held it as tight as you could, and cried over it, till the fellows helped you to the pump to wash the blood off. Then, as soon as you could, you limped home for a rag, and kept pretty quiet about it so as to get out again without letting on to your mother.

A MEAN TRICK

There were shade-trees all along the street, that you could climb if you wanted to, or that you could lie down under when you had run yourself out of breath, or play mumble-the-peg. My boy distinctly remembered that under one of these trees his elder brother first broached to him that awful scheme of reform about fibbing, and applied to their own lives the moral of *The Trippings of Tom Pepper;* he remembered how a conviction of the righteousness of the scheme sank into his soul, and he could not withhold his consent. Under the same tree, and very likely at the same time, a solemn conclave of boys, all the boys there were, discussed the feasibility of tying a tin can to a dog's tail, and seeing how he would act. They had all heard of the thing, but [Pg 94] none of them had seen it; and it was not so much a question of whether you ought to do a thing that on the very face of it would be so much fun, and if it did not amuse the dog as highly as anybody, could certainly do him no harm, as it was a question of whose dog you should get to take the dog's part in the sport. It was held that an old dog would probably not keep still long enough for you to tie the can on; he would have his suspicions; or else he would not run when the can was tied on, but very likely just go and lie down somewhere. The lot finally fell to a young yellow dog belonging to one of the boys, and the owner at once ran home to get him, and easily lured him back to the other boys with flatteries and caresses. The flatteries and caresses were not needed, for a dog is always glad to go with boys, upon any pretext, and so far from thinking that he does them a favor, he feels himself greatly honored. But I dare say the boy had a guilty fear that if his dog had known why he was invited to be of that party of boys, he might have pleaded a previous engagement. As it was, he came joyfully, and allowed the can to be tied to his tail without misgiving. If there had been any question with the boys as to whether he would enter fully into the spirit of the affair, it must have been instantly dissipated by the dogs behavior when he felt the loop tighten on [Pg 95] his tail, and looked round to see what the matter was. The boys hardly had a chance to cheer him before he flashed out of sight round the corner, and they hardly had time to think before he flashed into sight again from the other direction. He whizzed along the ground, and the can hurtled in the air, but there was no other sound, and the cheers died away on the boys' lips. The boy who owned the dog began to cry, and the other fellows began to blame him for not stopping the dog. But he might as well have tried to stop a streak of lightning; the only thing you could do was to keep out of the dog's way. As an experiment it was successful beyond the wildest dreams of its projectors, though it would have been a sort of relief if the dog had taken some other road, for variety, or had even reversed his course. But he kept on as he began, and by a common impulse the boys made up their minds to abandon the whole affair to him. They all ran home and hid, or else walked about and tried to ignore it. But at this point the grown-up people began to be interested; the mothers came to their doors to see what was the matter. Yet even the mothers were powerless in a case like that, and the enthusiast had to be left to his fate. He was found under a barn at last, breathless, almost lifeless, and he tried to bite the man who untied the can from his tail. Eventually he got well again, and [Pg 96] lived to be a solemn warning to the boys; he was touchingly distrustful of their advances for a time, but he finally forgot and forgave everything. They did not forget, and they never tried tying a tin can to a dog's tail again, among all the things they tried and kept trying. Once was enough; and they never even liked to talk of it, the sight was so awful. They were really fond of the dog, and if they could have thought he would take the matter so seriously, they would not have tried to have that kind of fun with him. It cured them of ever wanting to have that kind of fun with any dog.

TOPS

As the weather softened, tops came in some weeks after marbles went out, and just after foot-races were over, and a little before swimming began. At first the boys bought their tops at the stores, but after a while the boy whose father had the turning-shop on the Hydraulic learned to turn their tops, and did it for nothing, which was cheaper than buying tops, especially as he furnished the wood, too, and you only had to get the metal peg yourself. I believe he was the same boy who wanted to be a pirate and ended by inventing a steam-governor. He was very ingenious, and he knew how to turn a top out of [Pg 97] beech or maple that would outspin anything you could get in a store. The boys usually chose a firm, smooth piece of sidewalk, under one of the big trees in the Smith neighborhood, and spun their tops there. A fellow launched his top into the ring, and the rest waited till it began to go to sleep—that is, to settle in one place, and straighten up and spin silently, as if standing still. Then any fellow had a right to peg at it with his top, and if he hit it, he won it; and if he split it, as sometimes happened, the fellow that owned it had to give him a top. The boys came with their pockets bulged out with tops, but before long they had to go for more tops to that boy who could turn them. From this it was but another step to go to the shop with him and look on while he turned the tops; and then in process of time the boys discovered that the smooth floor of the shop was a better place to fight tops than the best piece of sidewalk. They would have given whole Saturdays to the sport there, but when they got to holloing too loudly the boy's father would come up, and then they would all run. It was considered mean in him, but the boy himself was awfully clever, and the first thing the fellows knew they were back there again. Some few of the boys had humming-tops, but though these pleased by their noise, they were not much esteemed, and could make no head [Pg 98] against the good old turnip-shaped tops, solid and weighty, that you could wind up with a stout cotton cord, and launch with perfect aim from the flat button held between your forefinger and middle finger. Some of the boys had a very pretty art in the twirl they gave the top, and could control its course, somewhat as a skilful pitcher can govern that of a baseball.

KITES

I do not know why a certain play went out, but suddenly the fellows who had been playing ball, or marbles, or tops, would find themselves playing something else. Kites came in just about the time of the greatest heat in summer, and lasted a good while; but could not have lasted as long as the heat, which began about the first of June, and kept on well through September; no play could last so long as that, and I suppose kite-flying must have died into swimming after the Fourth of July. The kites were of various shapes: bow kites, two-stick kites, and house kites. A bow kite could be made with half a barrel hoop carried over the top of a cross, but it was troublesome to make, and it did not fly very well, and somehow it was thought to look babyish; but it was held in greater respect than the [Pg 99] two-stick kite, which only the smallest boys played with, and which was made by fastening two sticks in the form of a cross. Any fellow more than six years old who appeared on the Commons with a two-stick kite would have been met with jeers, as a kind of girl.

The favorite kite, the kite that balanced best, took the wind best, and flew best, and that would stand all day when you got it up, was the house kite, which was made of three sticks, and shaped nearly in the form of the gable of a gambrel-roofed house, only smaller at the base than at the point where the roof would begin. The outline of all these kites was given, and the sticks stayed in place by a string carried taut from stick to stick, which was notched at the ends to hold it; sometimes the sticks were held with a tack at the point of crossing, and sometimes they were mortised into one another; but this was apt to weaken them. The frame was laid down on a sheet of paper, and the paper was cut an inch or two larger, and then pasted and folded over the string. Most of the boys used a paste made of flour and cold water; but my boy and his brother could usually get paste from the printing-office; and when they could not they would make it by mixing flour and water cream-thick, and slowly boiling it. That was a paste that would hold till the cows came [Pg 100] home, the boys said, and my boy was courted for his skill in making it. But after the kite was pasted, and dried in the sun, or behind the kitchen stove, if you were in very much of a hurry (and you nearly always were), it had to be hung, with belly-bands and tail-bands; that is, with strings carried from stick to stick over the face and at the bottom, to attach the cord for flying it and to fasten on the tail by. This took a good deal of art, and unless it were well done the kite would not balance, but would be always pitching and darting. Then the tail had to be of just the right weight; if it was too heavy the kite kept sinking, even after you got it up where otherwise it would stand; if too light, the kite would dart, and dash itself to pieces on the ground. A very pretty tail was made by tying twists of paper across a string a foot apart, till there were enough to balance the kite; but this sort of tail was apt to get tangled, and the best tail was made of a long streamer of cotton rags, with a gay tuft of dog-fennel at the end. Dog-fennel was added or taken away till just the right weight was got; and when this was done, after several experimental tests, the kite was laid flat on its face in the middle of the road, or on a long stretch of smooth grass; the bands were arranged, and the tail stretched carefully out behind, where it would not catch on bushes. [Pg 101] You unwound a great length of twine, running backward, and letting the twine slip swiftly through your hands till you had run enough out; then you seized the ball, and with one look over your shoulder to see that all was right, started swiftly forward. The kite reared itself from the ground, and swaying gracefully from side to side, rose slowly into the air, with its long tail climbing after it till the fennel tuft swung free. If there was not much surface wind you might have to run a little way, but as soon as the kite caught the upper currents it straightened itself, pulled the twine taut, and steadily mounted, while you gave it more and more twine; if the breeze was strong, the cord burned as it ran through your hands; till at last the kite stood still in the sky, at such a height that the cord holding it sometimes melted out of sight in the distance.

If it was a hot July day the sky would be full of kites, and the Commons would be dotted over with boys holding them, or setting them up, or winding them in, and all talking and screaming at the tops of their voices under the roasting sun. One might think that kite-flying, at least, could be carried on quietly and peaceably; but it was not. Besides the wild debate of the rival excellences of the different kites, there were always quarrels from getting the strings crossed; for, as the boys [Pg 102] got their kites up, they drew together for company and for an easier comparison of their merits. It was only a mean boy who would try to cross another fellow's string; but sometimes accidents would happen; two kites would become entangled and both would have to be hauled in, while their owners cried and scolded, and the other fellows cheered and laughed. Now and then the tail of a kite would part midway, and then the kite would begin to dart violently from side to side, and then to whirl round and round in swifter and narrower circles till it dashed itself to the ground. Sometimes the kite-string would break, and the kite would waver and fall like a bird shot in the wing; and the owner of the kite, and all the fellows who had no kites, would run to get it where it came down, perhaps a mile or more away. It usually came down in a tree, and they had to climb for it; but sometimes it lodged so high that no one could reach it; and then it was slowly beaten and washed away in the winds and rains, and its long tail left streaming all winter from the naked bough where it had caught. It was so good for kites on the Commons, because there were no trees there, and not even fences, but a vast open stretch of level grass, which the cows and geese kept cropped to the earth; and for the most part the boys had no trouble with their kites there. Some of them had paper fringe pasted [Pg 103] round the edges of their kites; this made a fine rattling as the kite rose, and when the kite stood, at the end of its string, you could hear the humming if you put your ear to the twine. But the most fun was sending up messengers. The messengers were cut out of thick paper, with a slit at one side, so as to slip over the string, which would be pulled level long enough to give the messenger a good start, and then released, when the wind would catch the little circle, and drive it up the long curving incline till it reached the kite.

It was thought a great thing in a kite to pull, and it was a favor to another boy to let him take hold of your string and feel how your kite pulled. If you wanted to play mumble-the-peg, or anything, while your kite was up, you tied it to a stake in the ground, or gave it to some other fellow to hold; there were always lots of fellows eager to hold it. But you had to be careful how you let a little fellow hold it; for, if it was a very powerful kite, it would take him up. It was not certain just how strong a kite had to be to take a small boy up, and nobody had ever seen a kite do it, but everybody expected to see it.

THE BUTLER GUARDS

The Butler Guards were the finest military company in the world. I do not believe there [Pg 104] was a fellow in the Boy's Town who even tried to imagine a more splendid body of troops: when they talked of them, as they did a great deal, it was simply to revel in the recognition of their perfection. I forget just what their uniform was, but there were white pantaloons in it, and a tuft of white-and-red cockerel plumes that almost covered the front of the hat, and swayed when the soldier walked, and blew in the wind. I think the coat was gray, and the skirts were buttoned back with buff, but I will not be sure of this; and somehow I cannot say how the officers differed from the privates in dress; it was impossible for them to be more magnificent. They walked backward in front of the platoons, with their swords drawn, and held in their white-gloved hands at hilt and point, and kept holloing, "Shoulder-r-r—arms! Carry—arms! Present—arms!" and then faced round, and walked a few steps forward, till they could think of something else to make the soldiers do. [Pg 105]

THE BUTLER GUARDS

[Pg 107]

Every boy intended to belong to the Butler Guards when he grew up; and he would have given anything to be the drummer or the marker. These were both boys, and they were just as much dressed up as the Guards themselves, only they had caps instead of hats with plumes. It was strange that the other fellows somehow did not know who these boys were; but they never knew, or at least my boy never knew. They thought more of the marker than of the drummer; for the marker carried a little flag, and when the officers holloed out, "By the left flank—left! Wheel!" he set his flag against his shoulder, and stood marking time with his feet till the soldiers all got by him, and then he ran up to the front rank, with the flag fluttering behind him. The fellows used to wonder how he got to be marker, and to plan how they could get to be markers in other companies, if not in the Butler Guards. There were other companies that used to come to town on the Fourth of July and Muster Day, from smaller places round about; and some of them had richer uniforms: one company had blue coats with gold epaulets, and gold braid going down in loops on the sides of their legs; all the soldiers, of course, had braid straight down the outer seams of their pantaloons. One Muster Day a captain of one of the country companies came home with my boy's father to dinner; he was in full uniform, and he put his plumed helmet down on the entry table just like any other hat.

There was a company of Germans, or Dutchmen, as the boys always called them; and the boys believed that they each had hay in his right shoe, and straw in his left, because a Dutchman was too dumb, as the boys said for stupid, to know his feet apart any other way; and that the [Pg 108] Dutch officers had to call out to the men when they were marching, "Up mit de hay-foot, down mit de straw-foot—*links, links, links!*" (left, left, left!). But the boys honored even these imperfect intelligences so much in their quality of soldiers that they would any of them have been proud to be marker in the Dutch company; and they followed the Dutchmen round in their march as fondly as any other body of troops. Of course, school let out when there was a regular muster, and the boys gave the whole day to it; but I do not know just when the Muster Day came. They fired the cannon a good deal on the river-bank, and they must have camped somewhere near the town, though no recollection of tents remained in my boy's mind. He believed with the rest of the boys that the right way to fire the cannon was to get it so hot you need not touch it off, but just keep your thumb on the touch-hole, and take it away when you wanted the cannon to go off. Once he saw the soldiers ram the piece full of dog-fennel on top of the usual charge, and then he expected the cannon to burst. But it only roared away as usual.

PETS

As there are no longer any Whig boys in the world, the coon can no longer be kept anywhere [Pg 109] as a political emblem, I dare say. Even in my boy's time the boys kept coons just for the pleasure of it, and without meaning to elect Whig governors and presidents with them. I do not know how they got them—they traded for them, perhaps, with fellows in the country that had caught them, or perhaps their fathers bought them in market; some people thought they were very good to eat, and, like poultry and other things for the table, they may have been brought alive to market. But, anyhow, when a boy had a coon, he had to have a store-box turned open side down to keep it in, behind the house; and he had to have a little door in the box to pull the coon out through when he wanted to show it to other boys, or to look at it himself, which he did [Pg 110]

forty or fifty times a day, when he first got it. He had to have a small collar for the coon, and a little chain, because the coon would gnaw through a string in a minute. The coon himself never seemed to take much interest in keeping a coon, or to see much fun or sense in it. He liked to stay inside his box, where he had a bed of hay, and whenever the boy pulled him out, he did his best to bite the boy. He had no tricks; his temper was bad; and there was nothing about him except the rings round his tail and his political principles that anybody could care for. He never did anything but bite, and try to get away, or else run back into his box, which smelled, pretty soon, like an animal-show; he would not even let a fellow see him eat.

My boy's brother had a coon, which he kept a good while, at a time when there was no election, for the mere satisfaction of keeping a coon. During his captivity the coon bit his keeper repeatedly through the thumb, and upon the whole seemed to prefer him to any other food; I do not really know what coons eat in a wild state, but this captive coon tasted the blood of nearly that whole family of children. Besides biting and getting away, he never did the slightest thing worth remembering; as there was no election, he did not even take part in a Whig procession. He got away two or three times. The first thing [Pg 111] his owner would know when he pulled the chain out was that there was no coon at the end of it, and then he would have to poke round the inside of the box pretty carefully with a stick, so as not to get bitten; after that he would have to see which tree the coon had gone up. It was usually the tall locust-tree in front of the house, and in about half a second all the boys in town would be there, telling the owner of the coon how to get him. Of course the only way was to climb for the coon, which would be out at the point of a high and slender limb, and would bite you awfully, even if the limb did not break under you, while the boys kept whooping and yelling and holloing out what to do, and Tip the dog just howled with excitement. I do not know how that coon was ever caught, but I know that the last time he got away he was not found during the day, but after nightfall he was discovered by moonlight in the locust-tree. His owner climbed for him, but the coon kept shifting about, and getting higher and higher, and at last he had to be left till morning. In the morning he was not there, nor anywhere.

It had been expected, perhaps, that Tip would watch him, and grab him if he came down, and Tip would have done it probably if he had kept awake. He was a dog of the greatest courage, and he was especially fond of hunting. He had [Pg 112] been bitten oftener by that coon than anybody but the coon's owner, but he did not care for biting. He was always getting bitten by rats, but he was the greatest dog for rats that there almost ever was. The boys hunted rats with him at night, when they came out of the stables that backed down to the Hydraulic, for water; and a dog who liked above all things to lie asleep on the back-step, by day, and would no more think of chasing a pig out of the garden than he would think of sitting up all night with a coon, would get frantic about rats, and would perfectly wear himself out hunting them on land and in the water, and keep on after the boys themselves were tired. He was so fond of hunting, anyway, that the sight of a gun would drive him about crazy; he would lick the barrel all over, and wag his tail so hard that it would lift his hind legs off the ground.

I do not know how he came into that family, but I believe he was given to it full grown by somebody. It was some time after my boy failed to buy what he called a Confoundland dog, from a colored boy who had it for sale, a pretty puppy with white and black spots which he had quite set his heart on; but Tip more than consoled him. Tip was of no particular breed, and he had no personal beauty; he was of the color of a mouse or an elephant, and his tail was without the smallest [Pg 113] grace; it was smooth and round, but it was so strong that he could pull a boy all over the town by it, and usually did; and he had the best, and kindest, and truest ugly old face in the world. He loved the whole human race, and as a watch-dog he was a failure through his trustful nature; he would no more have bitten a person than he would have bitten a pig; but where other dogs were concerned, he was a lion. He might be lying fast asleep in the back-yard, and he usually was, but if a dog passed the front of the house under a wagon, he would be up and after that dog before you knew what you were about. He seemed to want to fight country dogs the worst, but any strange dog would do. A good half the time he would come off best; but, however he came off, he returned to the back-yard with his tongue hanging out, and wagging his tail in good-humor with all the world. Nothing could stop him, however, where strange dogs were concerned. He was a Whig dog, of course, as any one could tell by his name, which was Tippecanoe in full, and was given him because it was the nickname of General Harrison, the great Whig who won the battle of Tippecanoe. The boys' Henry Clay Club used him to pull the little wagon that they went about in singing Whig songs, and he would pull five or six boys, guided simply by a stick which he held in his mouth, and [Pg 114] which a boy held on either side of him. But if he caught sight of a dog that he did not know, he would drop that stick and start for that dog as far off as he could see him, spilling the Henry Clay Club out of the wagon piecemeal as he went, and never stopping till he mixed up the strange dog in a fight where it would have been hard to tell which was either champion and which was the club wagon. When the fight was over Tip would come smilingly back to the fragments of the Henry Clay Club, with pieces of the vehicle sticking about him, and profess himself, in a dog's way, ready to go on with the concert.

Any crowd of boys could get Tip to go off with them, in swimming, or hunting, or simply running races. He was known through the whole town, and beloved for his many endearing qualities of heart. As to his mind, it was perhaps not much to brag of, and he certainly had some defects of character. He was incurably lazy, and his laziness grew upon him as he grew older, till hardly anything but the sight of a gun or a bone would move him. He lost his interest in politics, and, though there is no reason to suppose that he ever became indifferent to his principles, it is certain that he no longer showed his early ardor. He joined the Free-Soil movement in 1848, and supported Van Buren and Adams, [Pg 115] but without the zeal he had shown for Henry Clay. Once a year, as long as the family lived in the Boy's Town, the children were anxious about Tip when the dog-law was put in force, and the constables went round shooting all the dogs that were found running at large without muzzles. At this time, when Tip was in danger of going mad and biting people, he showed a most unseasonable activity, and could hardly be kept in bounds. A dog whose sole delight at other moments was to bask in the summer sun, or dream by the winter fire, would now rouse himself to an interest in everything that was going on in the dangerous world, and make forays into it at all unguarded points. The only thing to do was to muzzle him, and this was done by my boy's brother with a piece of heavy twine, in such a manner as to interfere with Tip's happiness as little as possible. It was a muzzle that need not be removed for either eating, drinking, or fighting; but it satisfied the law, and Tip always came safely through the dog-days, perhaps by favor or affection with the officers who were so inexorable with some dogs.

While Tip was still in his prime the family of children was further enriched by the possession of a goat; but this did not belong to the whole family, or it was, at least nominally, the property of that eldest brother they all looked up to. I [Pg 116] do not know how they came by the goat, any more than I know how they came by Tip; I only know that there came a time when it was already in the family, and that before it was got rid of it was a presence there was no mistaking. Nobody who has not kept a goat can have any notion of how many different kinds of mischief a goat can get into, without seeming to try, either, but merely by following the impulses of its own goatishness. This one was a nanny-goat, and it answered to the name of Nanny with an intelligence that was otherwise wholly employed in making trouble. It went up and down stairs, from cellar to garret, and in and out of all the rooms, like anybody, with a faint, cynical indifference in the glance of its cold gray eyes that gave no hint of its purposes or performances. In the chambers it chewed the sheets and pillow-cases on the beds, and in the dining-room, if it found nothing else, it would do its best to eat the table-cloth. Washing-day was a perfect feast for it, for then it would banquet on the shirt-sleeves and stockings that dangled from the clothes-line, and simply glut itself with the family linen and cotton. In default of these dainties, Nanny would gladly eat a chip-hat; she was not proud; she would eat a split-basket, if there was nothing else at hand. Once she got up on the kitchen table, and had a perfect orgy with a lot [Pg 117] of fresh-baked pumpkin-pies she found there; she cleaned all the pumpkin so neatly out of the pastry shells that, if there had been any more pumpkin left, they could have been filled up again, and nobody could have told the difference. The grandmother, who was visiting in the house at the time, declared to the mother that it would serve the father and the boys just right if she did fill these very shells up and give them to the father and the boys to eat. But I believe this was not done, and it was only suggested in a moment of awful exasperation, and because it was the father who was to blame for letting the boys keep the goat. The mother was always saying that the goat should not stay in the house another day, but she had not the heart to insist on its banishment, the children were so fond of it. I do not know why they were fond of it, for it never showed them the least affection, but was always taking the most unfair advantages of them, and it would butt them over whenever it got the chance. It would try to butt them into the well when they leaned down to pull up the bucket from the curb; and if it came out of the house, and saw a boy cracking nuts at the low flat stone the children had in the back-yard to crack nuts on, it would pretend that the boy was making motions to insult it, and before he knew what he was about it would fly at him and send him spinning head [Pg 118] over heels. It was not of the least use in the world, and could not be, but the children were allowed to keep it till, one fatal day, when the mother had a number of other ladies to tea, as the fashion used to be in small towns, when they sat down to a comfortable gossip over dainty dishes of stewed chicken, hot biscuit, peach-preserves, sweet tomato-pickles, and pound-cake. That day they all laid off their bonnets on the hall table, and the goat, after demurely waiting and watching with its faded eyes, which saw everything and seemed to see nothing, discerned a golden opportunity, and began to make such a supper of bonnet-ribbons as perhaps never fell to a goat's lot in life before. It was detected in its stolen joys just as it had chewed the ribbon of a best bonnet up to the bonnet, and was chased into the back-yard; but, as it had swallowed the ribbon without being able to swallow the bonnet, it carried that with it. The boy who specially owned the goat ran it down in a frenzy of horror and apprehension, and managed to unravel the ribbon from its throat, and get back the bonnet. Then he took the bonnet in and laid it carefully down on the table again, and decided that it would be best not to say anything about the affair. But such a thing as that could not be kept. The goat was known at once to have done the mischief; and this time it was really sent away. All [Pg 119] the children mourned it, and the boy who owned it the most used to go to the house of the people who took it, and who had a high board fence round their yard, and try to catch sight of it through the cracks. When he called "Nanny!" it answered him instantly with a plaintive "Baa!" and then, after a vain interchange of lamentations, he had to come away, and console himself as he could with the pets that were left him.

But all were trifling joys, except maybe Tip and Nanny, compared with the pony which the boys owned in common, and which was the greatest thing that ever came into their lives. I cannot tell just how their father came to buy it for them, or where he got it; but I dare say he thought they were about old enough for a pony, and might as well have one. It was a Mexican pony, and as it appeared on the scene just after the Mexican war, some volunteer may have brought it home. One volunteer brought home a Mexican dog, that was smooth and hairless, with a skin like an elephant, and that was always shivering round with the cold; he was not otherwise a remarkable dog, and I do not know that he ever felt even the warmth of friendship among the boys; his manners were reserved and his temper seemed doubtful. But the pony never had any trouble with the climate of Southern Ohio (which is indeed hot enough to fry a salamander in summer); [Pg 120] and though his temper was no better than other ponies', he was perfectly approachable. I mean that he was approachable from the side, for it was not well to get where he could bite you or kick you. He was of a bright sorrel color, and he had a brand on one haunch.

My boy had an ideal of a pony, conceived from pictures in his reading-books at school, that held its head high and arched its neck, and he strove by means of checks and martingales to make this real pony conform to the illustrations. But it was of no use; the real pony held his neck straight out like a ewe, or, if reined up, like a camel, and he hung his big head at the end of it with no regard whatever for the ideal. His caparison was another mortification and failure. What the boy wanted was an English saddle, embroidered on the morocco seat in crimson silk, and furnished with shining steel stirrups. What he had was the framework of a Mexican saddle, covered with rawhide, and cushioned with a blanket; the stirrups were Mexican, too, and clumsily fashioned out of wood. The boys were always talking about getting their father to get them a pad, but they never did it, and they managed as they could with the saddle they had. For the most part they preferred to ride the pony barebacked, for then they could ride him double, and when they [Pg 121] first got him they all wanted to ride him so much that they had to ride him double. They kept him going the whole day long; but after a while they calmed down enough to take him one at a time, and to let him have a chance for his meals.

They had no regular stable, and the father left the boys to fit part of the cow-shed up for the pony, which they did by throwing part of the hen-coop open into it. The pigeon-cots were just over his head, and he never could have complained of being lonesome. At first everybody wanted to feed him as well as ride him, and if he had been allowed time for it he might have eaten himself to death, or if he had not always tried to bite you or kick you when you came in with his corn. After a while the boys got so they forgot him, and nobody wanted to go out and feed the pony, especially after dark; but he knew how to take care of himself, and when he had eaten up everything there was in the cow-shed he would break out and eat up everything there was in the yard.

The boys got lots of good out of him. When you were once on his back you were pretty safe, for he was so lazy that he would not think of running away, and there was no danger unless he bounced you off when he trotted; he had a hard trot. The boys wanted to ride him standing [Pg 122] up, like circus-actors, and the pony did not mind, but the boys could not stay on, though they practised a good deal, turn about, when the other fellows were riding their horses, standing up, on the Commons. He was not of much use in Indian fights, for he could seldom be lashed into a gallop, and a pony that proposed to walk through an Indian fight was ridiculous. Still, with the help of imagination, my boy employed him in some scenes of wild Arab life, and hurled the Moorish javelin from him in mid-career, when the pony was flying along at the mad pace of a canal-boat. The pony early gave the boys to understand that they could get very little out of him in the way of herding the family cow. He would let them ride him to the pasture, and he would keep up with the cow on the way home, when she walked, but if they wanted anything more than that they must get some other pony. They tried to use him in carrying papers, but the subscribers objected to having him ridden up to their front doors over the sidewalk, and they had to give it up.

When he became an old story, and there was no competition for him among the brothers, my boy sometimes took him into the woods, and rode him in the wandering bridle-paths, with a thrilling sense of adventure. He did not like to be alone there, and he oftener had the company of [Pg 123] a boy who was learning the trade in his father's printing-office. This boy was just between him and his elder brother in age, and he was the good comrade of both; all the family loved him, and made him one of them, and my boy was fond of him because they had some tastes in common that were not very common among the other boys. They liked the same books, and they both began to write historical romances. My boy's romance was founded on facts of the Conquest of Granada, which he had read of again and again in Washington Irving, with a passionate pity for the Moors, and yet with pride in the grave and noble Spaniards. He would have given almost anything to be a Spaniard, and he lived in a dream of some day sallying out upon the Vega before Granada, in silk and steel, with an Arabian charger under him that champed its bit. In the mean time he did what he could with the family pony, and he had long rides in the woods with the other boy, who used to get his father's horse when he was not using it on Sunday, and race with him through the dangling wild grape-vines and pawpaw thickets, and over the reedy levels of the river, their hearts both bounding with the same high hopes of a world that could never come true. [Pg 124]

INDIANS

There was not a boy in the Boy's Town who would not gladly have turned from the town and lived in the woods if his mother had let him; and in every vague plan of running off the forest had its place as a city of refuge from pursuit and recapture. The pioneer days were still so close to those times that the love of solitary adventure which took the boys' fathers into the sylvan wastes of the great West might well have burned in the boys' hearts; and if their ideal of life was the free life of the woods, no doubt it was because their near ancestors had lived it. At any rate, that was their ideal, and they were always talking among themselves of how they would go farther West when they grew up, and be trappers and hunters. I do not remember any boy but one who meant to be a sailor; they lived too hopelessly far from the sea; and I dare say the boy who invented the marine-engine governor, and who wished to be a pirate, would just as soon have been a bandit of the Osage. In those days Oregon had just been opened to settlers, and the boys all wanted to go and live in Oregon, where you could stand in your door and shoot deer and wild turkey, while a salmon big enough to pull you in was tugging away at the line you had set in the river that ran before the log-cabin. [Pg 125]

If they could, the boys would rather have been Indians than anything else, but, as there was really no hope of this whatever, they were willing to be settlers, and fight the Indians. They had rather a mixed mind about them in the mean time, but perhaps they were not unlike other idolaters in both fearing and adoring their idols; perhaps they came pretty near being Indians in that, and certainly they came nearer than they knew. When they played war, and the war was between the whites and the Indians, it was almost as low a thing to be white as it was to be British when there were Americans on the other side; in either case you had to be beaten. The boys lived in the desire, if not the hope, of some time seeing an Indian, and they made the most of the Indians in the circus, whom they knew to be just white men dressed up; but none of them dreamed that what really happened one day could ever happen. This was at the arrival of several canal-boat loads of genuine Indians from the Wyandot Reservation in the northwestern part of the State, on their way to new lands beyond the Mississippi. The boys' fathers must have known that these Indians were coming, but it just shows how stupid the most of fathers are, that they never told the boys about it. All at once there the Indians were, as if the canal-boats had dropped with them out of heaven. There [Pg 126] they were, crowding the decks, in their blankets and moccasins, braves and squaws and pappooses, standing about or squatting in groups, not saying anything, and looking exactly like the pictures. The squaws had the pappooses on their backs, and the men and boys had bows and arrows in their hands; and as soon as the boats landed the Indians, all except the squaws and pappooses, came ashore, and went up to the courthouse yard, and began to shoot with their bows and arrows. It almost made the boys crazy. [Pg 127]

ALL AT ONCE THERE THE INDIANS WERE

Of course they would have liked to have the Indians shoot at birds, or some game, but they were mighty glad to have them shoot at cents and bits and quarters that anybody could stick up in the ground. The Indians would all shoot at the mark till some one hit it, and the one who hit it had the money, whatever it was. The boys ran and brought back the arrows; and they were so proud to do this that I wonder they lived through it. My boy was too bashful to bring the Indians their arrows; he could only stand apart and long to approach the filthy savages, whom he revered; to have touched the border of one of their blankets would have been too much. Some of them were rather handsome, and two or three of the Indian boys were so pretty that the Boy's Town boys said they were girls. They were of all ages, from old, withered men to children of six or seven, but [Pg 129] they were all alike grave and unsmiling; the old men were not a whit more dignified than the children, and the children did not enter into their sport with more zeal and ardor than the wrinkled sages who shared it. In fact they were, old and young alike, savages, and the boys who looked on and envied them were savages in their ideal of a world where people spent their lives in hunting and fishing and ranging the woods, and never grew up into the toils and cares that can alone make men of boys. They wished to escape these, as many foolish persons do among civilized nations, and they thought if they could only escape them they would be happy; they did not know that they would be merely savage, and that the great difference between a savage and a civilized man is work. They would all have been willing to follow these Indians away into the Far West, where they were going, and be barbarians for the rest of their days; and the wonder is that some of the fellows did not try it.

GUNS

After the red men had flitted away like red leaves, their memory remained with the boys, and a plague of bows and arrows raged among them, and it was a good while before they [Pg 130] calmed down to their old desire of having a gun. But they came back to that at last, for that was the normal desire of every boy in the Boy's Town who was not a girl-boy, and there were mighty few girl-boys there. Up to a certain point a pistol would do, especially if you had bullet-moulds, and could run bullets to shoot out of it; only your mother would be sure to see you running them, and just as likely as not would be so scared that she would say you must not shoot bullets. Then you would have to use buckshot, if you could get them anywhere near the right size, or small marbles; but a pistol was always a makeshift, and you never could hit anything with it, not even a board fence; it always kicked, or burst, or something.

Very few boys ever came to have a gun, though they all expected to have one. But seven or eight boys would go hunting with one shot-gun, and take turn-about shooting; some of the little fellows never got to shoot at all, but they could run and see whether the big boys had hit anything when they fired, and that was something. This was my boy's privilege for a long time before he had a gun of his own, and he went patiently with his elder brother, and never expected to fire the gun, except, perhaps, to shoot the load off before they got back to town; they were not allowed [Pg 131] to bring the gun home loaded. It was a gun that was pretty safe for anything in front of it, but you never could tell what it was going to do. It began by being simply an old gun-barrel, which my boy's brother bought of another boy who was sick of it for a fip, as the half-real piece was called, and it went on till it got a lock from one gunsmith and a stock from another, and was a complete gun. But this took time; perhaps a month; for the gunsmiths would only work at it in their leisure; they were delinquent subscribers, and they did it in part pay for their papers. When they got through with it my boy's brother made himself a ramrod out of a straight piece of hickory, or at least as straight as the gun-barrel, which was rather sway-backed, and had a little twist to one side, so that one of the jour printers said it was a first-rate gun to shoot round a corner with. Then he made himself a powder-flask out of an ox-horn that he got and boiled till it was soft (it smelt the whole house up), and then scraped thin with a piece of glass; it hung at his side; and he carried his shot in his pantaloons pocket. He went hunting with this gun for a good many years, but he had never shot anything with it, when his uncle gave him a smooth-bore rifle, and he in turn gave his gun to my boy, who must then have been nearly ten years old. [Pg 132]

It seemed to him that he was quite old enough to have a gun; but he was mortified the very next morning after he got it by a citizen who thought differently. He had risen at daybreak to go out and shoot kildees on the Common, and he was hurrying along with his gun on his shoulder when the citizen stopped him and asked him what he was going to do with that gun. He said to shoot kildees, and he added that it was his gun. This seemed to surprise the citizen even more than the boy could have wished. He asked him if he did not think he was a pretty small boy to have a gun; and he took the gun from him, and examined it thoughtfully, and then handed it back to the boy, who felt himself getting smaller all the time. The man went his way without saying anything more, but his behavior was somehow so sarcastic that the boy had no pleasure in his sport that morning; partly, perhaps, because he found no kildees to shoot at on the Common. He only fired off his gun once or twice at a fence, and then he sneaked home with it through alleys and by-ways, and whenever he met a person he hurried by for fear the person would find him too small to have a gun.

Afterward he came to have a bolder spirit about it, and he went hunting with it a good deal. It was a very curious kind of gun; you had to snap a good many caps on it, sometimes, before the [Pg 133] load would go off; and sometimes it would hang fire, and then seem to recollect itself, and go off, maybe, just when you were going to take it down from your shoulder. The barrel was so crooked that it could not shoot straight, but this was not the only reason why the boy never hit anything with it. He could not shut his left eye and keep his right eye open; so he had to take aim with both eyes, or else with the left eye, which was worse yet, till one day when he was playing shinny (or hockey) at school, and got a blow over his left eye from a shinny-stick. At first he thought his eye was put out; he could not see for the blood that poured into it from the cut above it. He ran homeward wild with fear, but on the way he stopped at a pump to wash away the blood, and then he found his eye was safe. It suddenly came into his mind to try if he could not shut that eye now, and keep the right one open. He found that he could do it perfectly; by help of his handkerchief, he stanched his wound, and made himself presentable, with the glassy pool before the pump for a mirror, and went joyfully back to school. He kept trying his left eye, to make sure it had not lost its new-found art, and as soon as school was out he hurried home to share the joyful news with his family.

He went hunting the very next Saturday, and at the first shot he killed a bird. It was a [Pg 134] suicidal sap-sucker, which had suffered him to steal upon it so close that it could not escape even the vagaries of that wandering gun-barrel, and was blown into such small pieces that the boy could bring only a few feathers of it away. In the evening, when his father came home, he showed him these trophies of the chase, and boasted of his exploit with the minutest detail. His father asked him whether he had expected to eat this sap-sucker, if he could have got enough of it together. He said no, sap-suckers were not good to eat. "Then you took its poor little life merely for the pleasure of killing it," said the father. "Was it a great pleasure to see it die?" The boy hung his head in shame and silence; it seemed to him that he would never go hunting again. Of course he did go hunting often afterward, but his brother and he kept faithfully to the rule of never killing anything that they did not want to eat. To be sure, they gave themselves a wide range; they were willing to eat almost anything that they could shoot, even blackbirds, which were so abundant and so easy to shoot. But there were some things which they would have thought it not only wanton but wicked to kill, like turtle-doves, which they somehow believed were sacred, nor robins either, because robins were hallowed by poetry, and they kept about the house, and [Pg 135] were almost tame, so that it seemed a shame to shoot them. They were very plentiful, and so were the turtle-doves, which used to light on the Basin bank, and pick up the grain scattered there from the boats and wagons.

There were a good many things you could do with a gun: you could fire your ramrod out of it, and see it sail through the air; you could fill the muzzle up with water, on top of a charge, and send the water in a straight column at a fence. The boys all believed that you could fire that column of water right through a man, and they always wanted to try whether it would go through a cow, but they were afraid the owner of the cow would find it out. There was a good deal of pleasure in cleaning your gun when it got so foul that your ramrod stuck in it and you could hardly get it out. You poured hot water into the muzzle and blew it through the nipple, till it began to show clear; then you wiped it dry with soft rags wound on your gun-screw, and then oiled it with greasy tow. Sometimes the tow would get loose from the screw, and stay in the barrel, and then you would have to pick enough powder in at the nipple to blow it out. Of course I am talking of the old muzzle-loading shot-gun, which I dare say the boys never use nowadays.

But the great pleasure of all, in hunting, was getting home tired and footsore in the evening, [Pg 136] and smelling the supper almost as soon as you came in sight of the house. There was nearly always hot biscuit for supper, with steak, and with coffee such as nobody but a boy's mother ever knew how to make; and just as likely as not there was some kind of preserves; at any rate, there was apple-butter. You could hardly take the time to wash the powder-grime off your hands and face before you rushed to the table; and if you had brought home a yellowhammer you left it with your gun on the back porch, and perhaps the cat got it and saved you the trouble of cleaning it. A cat can clean a bird a good deal quicker than a boy can, and she does not hate to do it half as badly.

Next to the pleasure of getting home from hunting late was the pleasure of starting early, as my boy and his brother sometimes did, to shoot ducks on the Little Reservoir in the fall. His brother had an alarm-clock, which he set at about four, and he was up the instant it rang, and pulling my boy out of bed, where he would rather have stayed than shot the largest mallard duck in the world. They raked the ashes off the bed of coals in the fireplace, and while the embers ticked and bristled, and flung out little showers of sparks, they hustled on their clothes, and ran down the back stairs into the yard with their guns. [Pg 137]

Tip, the dog, was already waiting for them there, for he seemed to know they were going that morning, and he began whimpering for joy, and twisting himself sideways up against them, and nearly wagging his tail off; and licking their hands and faces, and kissing their guns all over; he was about crazy. When they started, he knew where they were going, and he rushed ahead through the silent little sleeping town, and led the way across the wide Commons, where the cows lay in dim bulks on the grass, and the geese waddled out of his way with wild, clamorous cries, till they came in sight of the Reservoir. Then Tip fell back with my boy and let the elder brother go ahead, for he always had a right to the first shot; and while he dodged down behind the bank, and crept along to the place where the ducks usually were, my boy kept a hold on Tip's collar, and took in the beautiful mystery of the early morning. The place so familiar by day was estranged to his eyes in that pale light, and he was glad of old Tip's company, for it seemed a time when there might very well be ghosts about. The water stretched a sheet of smooth, gray silver, with little tufts of mist on its surface, and through these at last he could see the ducks softly gliding to and fro, and he could catch some dreamy sound from them. His heart stood still and then jumped wildly in his breast, as the still [Pg 138] air was startled with the rush of wings, and the water broke with the plunge of other flocks arriving. Then he began to make those bets with himself that a boy hopes he will lose: he bet that his brother would not hit any of them; he bet that he did not even see them; he bet that if he did see them and got a shot at them, they would not come back so that he could get a chance himself to kill any. It seemed to him that he had to wait an hour, and just when he was going to hollo, and tell his brother where the ducks were, the old smooth-bore sent out a red flash and a white puff before he heard the report; Tip tore loose from his grasp; and he heard the splashing rise of the ducks, and the hurtling rush of their wings; and he ran forward, yelling, "How many did you hit? Where are they? Where are you? Are they coming back? It's my turn now!" and making an outcry that would have frightened away a fleet of ironclads, but much less a flock of ducks.

One shot always ended the morning's sport, and there were always good reasons why this shot never killed anything.

NUTTING

The woods were pretty full of the kind of hickory-trees called pignuts, and the boys gathered [Pg 139] the nuts, and even ate their small, bitter kernels; and around the Poor-House woods there were some shag-barks, but the boys did not go for them because of the bull and the crazy people. Their great and constant reliance in foraging was the abundance of black walnuts which grew everywhere, along the roads and on the river-banks, as well as in the woods and the pastures. Long before it was time to go walnutting, the boys began knocking off the nuts and trying whether they were ripe enough; and just as soon as the kernels began to fill out, the fellows began making walnut wagons. I do not know why it was thought necessary to have a wagon to gather walnuts, but I know that it was, and that a boy had to make a new wagon every year.

No boy's walnut wagon could last till the next year; it did very well if it lasted till the next day. He had to make it nearly all with his pocket-knife. He could use a saw to block the wheels out of a pine board, and he could use a hatchet to rough off the corners of the blocks, but he had to use his knife to give them any sort of roundness, and they were not very round then; they were apt to be oval in shape, and they always wabbled. He whittled the axles out with his knife, and he made the hubs with it. He could get a tongue ready-made if he used a broom-handle [Pg 140] or a hoop-pole, but that had in either case to be whittled so it could be fastened to the wagon; he even bored the linchpin holes with his knife if he could not get a gimlet; and if he could not get an auger, he bored the holes through the wheels with a red-hot poker, and then whittled them large enough with his knife. He had to use pine for nearly everything, because any other wood was too hard to whittle; and then the pine was always splitting. It split in the axles when he was making the linchpin holes, and the wheels had to be kept on by linchpins that were tied in; the wheels themselves split, and had to be strengthened by slats nailed across the rifts. The wagon-bed was a candle-box nailed to the axles, and that kept the front axle tight, so that it took the whole width of a street to turn a very little wagon in without upsetting.

When the wagon was all done, the boy who owned it started off with his brothers, or some other boys who had no wagon, to gather walnuts. He started early in the morning of some bright autumn day while the frost still bearded the grass in the back-yard, and bristled on the fence-tops and the roof of the woodshed, and hurried off to the woods so as to get there before the other boys had got the walnuts. The best place for them was in some woods-pasture where the trees stood free of one another, and around them, in among the tall, frosty grass, the tumbled nuts lay scattered in groups of twos and threes, or fives, some still yellowish-green in their hulls, and some black, but all sending up to the nostrils of the delighted boy the incense of their clean, keen, wild-woody smell, to be a memory forever. [Pg 141]

NUTTING

[Pg 143]

The leaves had dropped from the trees overhead, and the branches outlined themselves against the blue sky, and dangled from their outer stems clusters of the unfallen fruit, as large as oranges, and only wanting a touch to send them plumping down into the grass where sometimes their fat hulls burst, and the nuts almost leaped into the boy's hands. The boys ran, some of them to gather the fallen nuts, and others to get clubs and rocks to beat them from the trees; one was sure to throw off his jacket and kick off his shoes and climb the tree to shake every limb where a walnut was still clinging. When they had got them all heaped up like a pile of grape-shot at the foot of the tree, they began to hull them, with blows of a stick, or with stones, and to pick the nuts from the hulls, where the grubs were battening on their assured ripeness, and to toss them into a little heap, a very little heap indeed compared with the bulk of that they came from. The boys gloried in getting as much walnut stain on their hands as they could, for it would not [Pg 144] wash off, and it showed for days that they had been walnutting; sometimes they got to staining one another's faces with the juice, and pretending they were Indians.

The sun rose higher and higher, and burned the frost from the grass, and while the boys worked and yelled and chattered they got hotter and hotter, and began to take off their shoes and stockings, till every one of them was barefoot. Then, about three or four o'clock, they would start homeward, with half a bushel of walnuts in their wagon, and their shoes and stockings piled in on top of them. That is, if they had good luck. In a story, they would always have had good luck, and always gone home with half a bushel of walnuts; but this is a history, and so I have to own that they usually went home with about two quarts of walnuts rattling round under their shoes and stockings in the bottom of the wagon. They usually had no such easy time getting them as they always would in a story; they did not find them under the trees, or ready to drop off, but they had to knock them off with about six or seven clubs or rocks to every walnut, and they had to pound the hulls so hard to get the nuts out that sometimes they cracked the nuts. That was because they usually went walnutting before the walnuts were ripe. But they made just as much preparation for drying the [Pg 145] nuts on the woodshed roof whether they got half a gallon or half a bushel; for they did not intend to stop gathering them till they had two or three barrels. They nailed a cleat across the roof to keep them from rolling off, and they spread them out thin, so that they could look more than they were, and dry better. They said they were going to keep them for Christmas, but they had to try pretty nearly every hour or so whether they were getting dry, and in about three days they were all eaten up.

THE FIRE-ENGINES

There were two fire-engines in the Boy's Town; but there seemed to be something always the matter with them, so that they would not work, if there was a fire. When there was no fire, the companies sometimes pulled them up through the town to the Basin bank, and practised with them against the roofs and fronts of the pork-houses. It was almost as good as a muster to see the firemen in their red shirts and black trousers, dragging the engine at a run, two and two together, one on each side of the rope.

My boy would have liked to speak to a fireman, but he never dared; and the foreman of the *Neptune*, [Pg 146] which was the larger and feebler of the engines, was a figure of such worshipful splendor in his eyes that he felt as if he could not be just a common human being. He was a storekeeper, to begin with, and he was tall and slim, and his black trousers fitted him like a glove; he had a patent-leather helmet, and a brass speaking-trumpet, and he gave all his orders through this. It did not make any difference how close he was to the men, he shouted everything through the trumpet; and when they manned the brakes and began to pump, he roared at them, "Down on her, down on her, boys!" so that you would have thought the *Neptune* could put out the world if it was burning up. Instead of that there was usually a feeble splutter from the nozzle, and sometimes none at all, even if the hose did not break; it was fun to see the hose break.

The *Neptune* was a favorite with the boys, though they believed that the *Tremont* could squirt farther, and they had a belief in its quiet efficiency which was fostered by its reticence in public. It was small and black, but the *Neptune* was large, and painted of a gay color lit up with gilding that sent the blood leaping through a boy's veins. The boys knew the *Neptune* was out of order, but they were always expecting it would come right, and in the mean time they felt that it was an honor to the town, and they followed [Pg 147] it as proudly back to the engine-house after one of its magnificent failures as if it had been a magnificent success. The boys were always making magnificent failures themselves, and they could feel for the *Neptune*.

[Pg 149]

IV

GLIMPSES OF THE LARGER WORLD

[Pg 151]

THE TRAVELLING CIRCUS

The boys made a very careful study of the circus bills, and when the circus came they held the performance to a strict account for any difference between the feats and their representation. For a fortnight beforehand they worked themselves up for the arrival of the circus into a fever of fear and hope, for it was always a question with a great many whether they could get their fathers to give them the money to go in. The full price was two bits, and the half-price was a bit, or a Spanish real, then a commoner coin than the American dime in the West; and every boy, for that time only, wished to be little enough to look young enough to go in for a bit. Editors of newspapers had a free ticket for every member of their families; and my boy was sure of going to the circus from the first rumor of its coming. But he was none the less deeply thrilled by the coming event, and he was up early on the morning of the great day, to go out and meet the circus procession beyond the corporation line.

I do not really know how boys live through the [Pg 152] wonder and the glory of such a sight. Once there were two chariots—one held the band in red-and-blue uniforms, and was drawn by eighteen piebald horses; and the other was drawn by a troop of Shetland ponies, and carried in a vast mythical sea-shell little boys in spangled tights and little girls in the gauze skirts and wings of fairies. There was not a flaw in this splendor to the young eyes that gloated on it, and that followed it in rapture through every turn and winding of its course in the Boy's Town; nor in the magnificence of the actors and actresses, who came riding two by two in their circus dresses after the chariots, and looking some haughty and contemptuous, and others quiet and even bored, as if it were nothing to be part of such a procession. The boys tried to make them out by the pictures and names on the bills: which was Rivers, the bareback-rider, and which was O'Dale, the champion tumbler; which was the India-rubber man, which the ring-master, which the clown.

Covered with dust, gasping with the fatigue of a three hours' run beside the procession, but fresh at heart as in the beginning, they arrived with it on the Commons, where the tent-wagons were already drawn up, and the ring was made, and mighty men were driving the iron-headed tent-stakes, and stretching the ropes of [Pg 153] the great skeleton of the pavilion which they were just going to clothe with canvas. The boys were not allowed to come anywhere near, except three or four who got leave to fetch water from a neighboring well, and thought themselves richly paid with half-price tickets. The other boys were proud to pass a word with them as they went by with their brimming buckets; fellows who had money to go in would have been glad to carry water just for the glory of coming close to the circus men. They stood about in twos and threes, and lay upon the grass in groups debating whether a tan-bark ring was better than a saw-dust ring; there were different opinions. They came as near the wagons as they dared, and looked at the circus horses munching hay from the tail-boards, just like common horses. The wagons were left standing outside of the tent; but when it was up, the horses were taken into the dressing-room, and then the boys, with many a backward look at the wide spread of canvas, and the flags and streamers floating over it from the centre-pole (the centre-pole was revered almost like a distinguished personage), ran home to dinner so as to get back good and early, and be among the first to go in.

All round, before the circus doors were open, the doorkeepers of the side-shows were inviting people to come in and see the giants and [Pg 154] fat woman and boa-constrictors, and there were stands for peanuts and candy and lemonade; the vendors cried, "Ice-cold lemonade, from fifteen hundred miles under ground! Walk up, roll up, tumble up, any way you get up!" The boys thought this brilliant drolling, but they had no time to listen after the doors were open, and they had no money to spend on side-shows or dainties anyway. Inside the tent they found it dark and cool, and their hearts thumped in their throats with the wild joy of being there; they recognized one another with amaze, as if they had not met for years, and the excitement kept growing as other fellows came in. It was lots of fun, too, watching the country-jakes, as the boys called the farmer-folk, and seeing how green they looked, and now some of them tried to act smart with the circus men that came round with oranges to sell. But the great thing was to see whether fellows that said they were going to hook in really got in. The boys held it to be a high and creditable thing to hook into a show of any kind, but hooking into a circus was something that a fellow ought to be held in special honor for doing. He ran great risks, and if he escaped the vigilance of the massive circus man who patrolled the outside of the tent with a cow-hide and a bulldog, perhaps he merited the fame he was sure to win. [Pg 155]

I do not know where boys get some of the notions of morality that govern them. These notions are like the sports and plays that a boy leaves off as he gets older to the boys that are younger. He outgrows them, and other boys grow into them, and then outgrow them as he did. Perhaps they come down to the boyhood of our time from the boyhood of the race, and the unwritten laws of conduct may have prevailed among the earliest Aryans on the plains of Asia that I now find so strange in a retrospect of the Boy's Town.

The standard of honor there was, in a certain way, very high among the boys; they would have despised a thief as he deserved, and I cannot remember one of them who might not have been safely trusted. None of them would have taken an apple out of a market-wagon, or stolen a melon from a farmer who came to town with it; but they would all have thought it fun, if not right, to rob an orchard or hook a watermelon out of a patch. This would have been a foray into the enemy's country, and the fruit of the adventure would have been the same as the plunder of a city, or the capture of a vessel belonging to him on the high seas. In the same way, if one of the boys had seen a circus man drop a quarter, he would have hurried to give it back to him, but he would only have been proud to hook into the circus man's show, and the other [Pg 156] fellows would have been proud of his exploit, too, as something that did honor to them all. As a person who enclosed bounds and forbade trespass, the circus man constituted himself the enemy of every boy who respected himself, and challenged him to practise any sort of strategy. There was not a boy in the crowd that my boy went with who would have been allowed to hook into a circus by his parents; yet hooking in was an ideal that was cherished among them, that was talked of, and that was even sometimes attempted, though not often. Once, when a fellow really hooked in, and joined the crowd that had ignobly paid, one of the fellows could not stand it. He asked him just how and where he got in, and then he went to the door, and got back his money from the doorkeeper upon the plea that he did not feel well; and in five or ten minutes he was back among the boys, a hero of such moral grandeur as would be hard to describe. Not one of the fellows saw him as he really was—a little lying, thievish scoundrel. Not even my boy saw him so, though he had on some other point of personal honesty the most fantastic scruples.

The boys liked to be at the circus early so as to make sure of the grand entry of the performers into the ring, where they caracoled round on horseback, and gave a delicious foretaste of the wonders to come. The fellows were united in [Pg 157] this, but upon other matters feeling varied—some liked tumbling best; some the slack-rope; some bareback-riding; some the feats of tossing knives and balls and catching them. There never was more than one ring in those days; and you were not tempted to break your neck and set your eyes forever askew, by trying to watch all the things that went on at once in two or three rings.

The boys did not miss the smallest feats of any performance, and they enjoyed them every one, not equally, but fully. They had their preferences, of course, as I have hinted; and one of the most popular acts was that where a horse has been trained to misbehave, so that nobody can mount him; and after the actors have tried him, the ring-master turns to the audience, and asks if some gentleman among them wants to try it. Nobody stirs, till at last a tipsy country-jake is seen making his way down from one of the top seats toward the ring. He can hardly walk, he is so drunk, and the clown has to help him across the ring-board, and even then he trips and rolls over on the saw-dust, and has to be pulled to his feet. When they bring him up to the horse, he falls against it; and the little fellows think he will certainly get killed. But the big boys tell the little fellows to shut up and watch out. The ring-master and the clown manage to get the country-jake on to the broad platform on the horse's back, [Pg 158] and then the ring-master cracks his whip, and the two supes who have been holding the horse's head let go, and the horse begins cantering round the ring. The little fellows are just sure the country-jake is going to fall off, he reels and totters so; but the big boys tell them to keep watching out; and pretty soon the country-jake begins to straighten up. He begins to unbutton his long gray overcoat, and then he takes it off and throws it into the ring, where one of the supes catches it. Then he sticks a short pipe into his mouth, and pulls on an old wool hat, and flourishes a stick that the supe throws to him, and you see that he is an Irishman just come across the sea; and then off goes another coat, and he comes out a British soldier in white duck trousers and red coat. That comes off, and he is an American sailor, with his hands on his hips, dancing a horn-pipe. Suddenly away flash wig and beard and false-face, the pantaloons are stripped off with the same movement, the actor stoops for the reins lying on the horse's neck, and James Rivers, the greatest three-horse rider in the world, nimbly capers on the broad pad, and kisses his hand to the shouting and cheering spectators as he dashes from the ring past the braying and bellowing brass-band into the dressing-room!

The big boys have known all along that he was not a real country-jake; but when the trained [Pg 159] mule begins, and shakes everybody off, just like the horse, and another country-jake gets up, and offers to bet that he can ride that mule, nobody can tell whether he is a real country-jake or not. This is always the last thing in the performance, and the boys have seen with heavy hearts many signs openly betokening the end which they knew was at hand. The actors have come out of the dressing-room door, some in their everyday clothes, and some with just overcoats on over their circus-dresses, and they lounge about near the bandstand watching the performance in the ring. Some of the people are already getting up to go out, and stand for this last act, and will not mind the shouts of "Down in front! Down there!" which the boys eagerly join in, to eke out their bliss a little longer by keeping away even the appearance of anything transitory in it. The country-jake comes stumbling awkwardly into the ring, but he is perfectly sober, and he boldly leaps astride the mule, which tries all its arts to shake him off, plunging, kicking, rearing. He sticks on, and everybody cheers him, and the owner of the mule begins to get mad and to make it do more things to shake the country-jake off. At last, with one convulsive spring, it flings him from its back, and dashes into the dressing-room, while the country-jake picks himself up and vanishes among the crowd. [Pg 160]

A man mounted on a platform in the ring is imploring the ladies and gentlemen to keep their seats, and to buy tickets for the negro-minstrel entertainment which is to follow, but which is not included in the price of admission. The boys would like to stay, but they have not the money, and they go out clamoring over the performance, and trying to decide which was the best feat. As to which was the best actor, there is never any question; it is the clown, who showed by the way he turned a double somersault that he can do anything, and who chooses to be clown simply because he is too great a creature to enter into rivalry with the other actors.

There will be another performance in the evening, with real fights outside between the circus men and the country-jakes, and perhaps some of the Basin rounders, but the boys do not expect to come; that would be too much. The boy's brother once stayed away in the afternoon, and went at night with one of the jour printers; but he was not able to report that the show was better than it was in the afternoon. He did not get home till nearly ten o'clock, though, and he saw the sides of the tent dropped before the people got out; that was a great thing; and what was greater yet, and reflected a kind of splendor on the boy at second hand, was that the jour printer and the clown turned out to be old friends. After [Pg 161] the circus, the boy actually saw them standing near the centre-pole talking together; and the next day the jour showed the grease that had dripped on his coat from the candles. Otherwise the boy might have thought it was a dream, that some one he knew had talked on equal terms with the clown. The boys were always intending to stay up and see the circus go out of town, and they would have done so, but their mothers would not let them. This may have been one reason why none of them ever ran off with a circus.

As soon as a circus had been in town, the boys began to have circuses of their own, and to practise for them. Everywhere you could see boys upside down, walking on their hands or standing on them with their legs dangling over, or stayed against house walls. It was easy to stand on your head; one boy stood on his head so much that he had to have it shaved, in the brain-fever that he got from standing on it; but that did not stop the other fellows. Another boy fell head downward from a rail where he was skinning-the-cat, and nearly broke his neck, and made it so sore that it was stiff ever so long. Another boy, who was playing Samson, almost had his leg torn off by the fellows that were pulling at it with a hook; and he did have the leg of his pantaloons torn off. Nothing could stop the boys but time, or some other play coming in; and circuses [Pg 162] lasted a good while. Some of the boys learned to turn hand-springs; anybody could turn cart-wheels; one fellow, across the river, could just run along and throw a somersault and light on his feet; lots of fellows could light on their backs; but if you had a spring-board, or shavings under a bank, like those by the turning-shop, you could practise for somersaults pretty safely.

All the time you were practising you were forming your circus company. The great trouble was not that any boy minded paying five or ten pins to come in, but that so many fellows wanted to belong there were hardly any left to form an audience. You could get girls, but even as spectators girls were a little *too* despicable; they did not know anything; they had no sense; if a fellow got hurt they cried. Then another thing was, where to have the circus. Of course it was simply hopeless to think of a tent, and a boy's circus was very glad to get a barn. The boy whose father owned the barn had to get it for the circus without his father knowing it; and just as likely as not his mother would hear the noise and come out and break the whole thing up while you were in the very middle of it. Then there were all sorts of anxieties and perplexities about the dress. You could do something by turning your roundabout inside out, and rolling your trousers up as far as they would go; but what a [Pg 163] fellow wanted to make him a real circus-actor was a long pair of white cotton stockings, and I never knew a fellow that got a pair; I heard of many a fellow who was said to have got a pair; but when you came down to the fact, they vanished like ghosts when you try to verify them. I believe the fellows always expected to get them out of a bureau-drawer or the clothes-line at home, but failed. In most other ways, a boy's circus was always a failure, like most other things boys undertake. They usually broke up under the strain of rivalry; everybody wanted to be the clown or ring-master; or else the boy they got the barn of behaved badly, and went into the house crying, and all the fellows had to run.

PASSING SHOWS

There were only two kinds of show known by that name in the Boy's Town: a nigger show, or [Pg 164] a performance of burnt-cork minstrels; and an animal show, or a strolling menagerie; and the boys always meant a menagerie when they spoke of a show, unless they said just what sort of show. The only perfect joy on earth in the way of an entertainment, of course, was a circus, but after the circus the show came unquestionably next. It made a processional entry into the town almost as impressive as the circus's, and the boys went out to meet it beyond the corporation line in the same way. It always had two elephants, at least, and four or five camels, and sometimes there was a giraffe. These headed the procession, the elephants in the very front, with their keepers at their heads, and then the camels led by halters dangling from their sneering lips and contemptuous noses. After these began to come the show-wagons, with pictures on their sides, very flattered portraits of the wild beasts and birds inside; lions first, then tigers (never meaner than Royal Bengal ones, which the boys understood to be a superior breed), then leopards, then pumas and panthers; then bears, then jackals and hyenas; then bears and wolves; then kangaroos, musk-oxen, deer, and such harmless cattle; and then ostriches, emus, lyre-birds, birds-of-Paradise, and all the rest.

From time to time the boys ran back from the elephants and camels to get what good they [Pg 165] could out of the scenes in which these hidden wonders were dramatized in acts of rapine or the chase, but they always came forward to the elephants and camels again. Even with them they had to endure a degree of denial, for although you could see most of the camels' figures, the elephants were so heavily draped that it was a kind of disappointment to look at them. The boys kept as close as they could, and came as near getting under the elephants' feet as the keepers would allow; but, after all, they were driven off a good deal and had to keep stealing back. They gave the elephants apples and bits of cracker and cake, and some tried to put tobacco into their trunks, though they knew very well that it was nearly certain death to do so; for any elephant that was deceived that way would recognize the boy that did it, and kill him the next time he came, if it was twenty years afterward. The boys used to believe that the Miami bridge would break down under the elephants if they tried to cross it, and they would have liked to see it do it, but no one ever saw it, perhaps because the elephants always waded the river. Some boys had seen them wading it, and stopping to drink and squirt the water out of their trunks. If an elephant got a boy that had given him tobacco into the river, he would squirt water on him till he drowned him. Still, some boys always tried to [Pg 166] give the elephants tobacco, just to see how they would act for the time being.

A show was not so much in favor as a circus, because there was so little performance in the ring. You could go round and look at the animals, mostly very sleepy in their cages, but you were not allowed to poke them through the bars, or anything; and when you took your seat there was nothing much till Herr Driesbach entered the lions' cage, and began to make them jump over his whip. It was some pleasure to see him put his head between the jaws of the great African King of Beasts, but the lion never did anything to him, and so the act wanted a true dramatic climax. The boys would really rather have seen a bareback-rider, like James Rivers, turn a back-somersault and light on his horse's crupper, any time, though they respected Herr Driesbach, too; they did not care much for a woman who once went into the lions' cage and made them jump round.

The boys had their own beliefs about the different animals, and one of these concerned the inappeasable ferocity of the zebra. I do not know why the zebra should have had this repute, for he certainly never did anything to deserve it; but, for the matter of that, he was like all the other animals. Bears were not much esteemed, but they would have been if they could have [Pg 167] been really seen hugging anybody to death. It was always hoped that some of the fiercest animals would get away and have to be hunted down, and retaken after they had killed a lot of dogs. If the elephants, some of them, had gone crazy, it would have been something, for then they would have roamed up and down the turnpike smashing buggies and wagons, and had to be shot with the six-pound cannon that was used to celebrate the Fourth of July with.

Another thing that was against the show was that the animals were fed after it was out, and you could not see the tigers tearing their prey when the great lumps of beef were thrown them. There was somehow not so much chance of hooking into a show as a circus, because the seats did not go all round, and you could be seen under the cages as soon as you got in under the canvas. I never heard of a boy that hooked into a show; perhaps nobody ever tried.

But the great reason of all was that you could not have an animal show of your own as you could a circus. You could not get the animals; and no boy living could act a camel, or a Royal Bengal tiger, or an elephant so as to look the least like one.

Of course you could have negro shows, and the boys often had them; but they were not much fun, and you were always getting the black on your shirt-sleeves. [Pg 168]

THE THEATRE COMES TO TOWN

A great new experience which now came to the boy was the theatre, which he had sometimes heard his father speak of. There had once been a theatre in the Boy's Town, when a strolling company came up from Cincinnati, and opened for a season in an empty pork-house. But that was a long time ago, and, though he had written a tragedy, all that the boy knew of a theatre was from a picture in a Sunday-school book where a stage scene was given to show what kind of desperate amusements a person might come to in middle life if he began by breaking the Sabbath in his youth. His brother had once been taken to a theatre in Pittsburg by one of their river-going uncles, and he often told about it; but my boy formed no conception of the beautiful reality from his accounts of a burglar who jumped from a roof and was chased by a watchman with a pistol up and down a street with houses painted on a curtain.

The company which came to the Boy's Town in his time was again from Cincinnati, and it was under the management of the father and mother of two actresses, afterward famous, who were then children, just starting upon their career. These pretty little creatures took the leading [Pg 169] parts in *Bombastes Furioso* the first night my boy ever saw a play, and he instantly fell impartially in love with both of them, and tacitly remained their abject slave for a great while after. When the smaller of them came out with a large pair of stage boots in one hand and a drawn sword in the other, and said:

"Whoever dares these boots displace
Shall meet Bombastes face to face,"

if the boy had not already been bereft of his senses by the melodrama preceding the burlesque, he must have been transported by her beauty, her grace, her genius. He, indeed, gave her and her sister his heart, but his mind was already gone, rapt from him by the adorable pirate who fought a losing fight with broadswords, two up and two down—click-click, click-click—and died all over the deck of the pirate ship in the opening piece. This was called the *Beacon of Death*, and the scene represented the forecastle of the pirate ship with a lantern dangling from the rigging, to lure unsuspecting merchantmen to their doom. Afterward the boy remembered nothing of the story, but a scrap of the dialogue meaninglessly remained with him; and when the pirate captain appeared with his bloody crew and said, hoarsely, "Let us go below and get some brandy!" the boy [Pg 170] would have bartered all his hopes of bliss to have been that abandoned ruffian. In fact, he always liked, and longed to be, the villain, rather than any other person in the play, and he so glutted himself with crime of every sort in his tender years at the theatre that he afterward came to be very tired of it, and avoided the plays and novels that had very marked villains in them.

He was in an ecstasy as soon as the curtain rose that night, and he lived somewhere out of his body as long as the playing lasted, which was well on to midnight; for in those days the theatre did not meanly put the public off with one play, but gave it a heartful and its money's worth with three. On his first night my boy saw *The Beacon of Death*, *Bombastes Furioso*, and *Black-Eyed Susan*, and he never afterward saw less than three plays each night, and he never missed a night, as long as the theatre languished in the unfriendly air of that mainly Calvinistic community, where the theatre was regarded by most good people as the eighth of the seven deadly sins. The whole day long he dwelt in a dream of it that blotted out, or rather consumed with more effulgent brightness, all the other day-dreams he had dreamed before, and his heart almost burst with longing to be a villain like those villains on the stage, to have a mustache—a black mustache—such as they wore at a time when every one off [Pg 171] the stage was clean shaven, and somehow to end bloodily, murderously, as became a villain.

I dare say this was not quite a wholesome frame of mind for a boy of ten years; but I do not defend it; I only portray it. Being the boy he was, he was destined somehow to dwell half the time in a world of dreamery; and I have tried to express how, when he had once got enough of villany, he reformed his ideals and rather liked virtue.

THE WORLD OPENED BY BOOKS

Every boy is two or three boys, or twenty or thirty different kinds of boys in one; he is all the time living many lives and forming many characters; but it is a good thing if he can keep one life and one character when he gets to be a man. He may turn out to be like an onion when he is grown up, and be nothing but hulls, that you keep peeling off, one after another, till you think you have got down to the heart, at last, and then you have got down to nothing.

All the boys may have been like my boy in the Boy's Town, in having each an inward being that was not the least like their outward being, but that somehow seemed to be their real self, whether it truly was so or not. But I am certain that this was the case with him, and that while [Pg 172] he was joyfully sharing the wild sports and conforming to the savage usages of the boy's world about him, he was dwelling in a wholly different world within him, whose wonders no one else knew. I could not tell now these wonders any more than he could have told them then; but it was a world of dreams, of hopes, of purposes, which he would have been more ashamed to avow for himself than I should be to avow for him. It was all vague and vast, and it came out of the books that he read, and that filled his soul with their witchery, and often held him aloof with their charm in the midst of the plays from which they could not lure him wholly away, or at all away. He did not know how or when their enchantment began, and he could hardly recall the names of some of them afterward.

First of them was Goldsmith's *History of Greece*, which made him an Athenian of Pericles' time, and Goldsmith's *History of Rome*, which naturalized him in a Roman citizenship chiefly employed in slaying tyrants; from the time of Appius Claudius down to the time of Domitian, there was hardly a tyrant that he did not slay. After he had read these books, not once or twice, but twenty times over, his father thought fit to put into his hands *The Travels of Captain Ashe in North America*, to encourage, or perhaps to test, his taste for useful [Pg 173] reading; but this was a failure. The captain's travels were printed with long esses, and the boy could make nothing of them, for other reasons. The fancy nourished upon

"The glory that was Greece
And the grandeur that was Rome,"

starved amid the robust plenty of the Englishman's criticisms of our early manners and customs. Neither could money hire the boy to read *Malte-Brun's Geography*, in three large folios, of a thousand pages each, for which there was a standing offer of fifty cents from the father, who had never been able to read it himself.

But shortly after he failed so miserably with Captain Ashe, the boy came into possession of a priceless treasure. It was that little treatise on *Greek and Roman Mythology* which I have mentioned, and which he must literally have worn out with reading, since no fragment of it seems to have survived his boyhood. Heaven knows who wrote it or published it; his father bought it with a number of other books at an auction, and the boy, who had about that time discovered the chapter on prosody in the back part of his grammar, made poems from it for years, and appeared in many transfigurations, as this and that god and demigod and hero upon imagined occasions in the Boy's Town, to the fancied admiration [Pg 174] of all the other fellows. I do not know just why he wished to appear to his grandmother in a vision; now as Mercury with winged feet, now as Apollo with his drawn bow, now as Hercules leaning upon his club and resting from his Twelve Labors. Perhaps it was because he thought that his grandmother, who used to tell the children about her life in Wales, and show them the picture of a castle where she had once slept when she was a girl, would appreciate him in these apotheoses. If he believed they would make a vivid impression upon the sweet old Quaker lady, no doubt he was right.

There was another book which he read about this time, and that was *The Greek Soldier*. It was the story of a young Greek, a glorious Athenian, who had fought through the Greek war of independence against the Turks, and then come to America and published the narrative of his adventures. They fired my boy with a retrospective longing to have been present at the Battle of Navarino, when the allied ships of the English, French, and Russians destroyed the Turkish fleet; but it seemed to him that he could not have borne to have the allies impose a king upon the Greeks, when they really wanted a republic, and so he was able to console himself for having been absent. He did what he could in fighting the war over again, and he intended [Pg 175] to harden himself for the long struggle by sleeping on the floor, as the Greek soldier had done. But the children often fell asleep on the floor in the warmth of the hearth-fire; and his preparation for the patriotic strife was not distinguishable in its practical effect from a reluctance to go to bed at the right hour.

Captain Riley's narrative of his shipwreck on the coast of Africa, and his captivity among the Arabs, was a book which my boy and his brother prized with a kind of personal interest, because their father told them that he had once seen a son of Captain Riley when he went to get his appointment of collector at Columbus, and that this son was named William Willshire Riley, after the good English merchant, William Willshire, who had ransomed Captain Riley.

William Willshire seemed to them almost the best man who ever lived; though my boy had secretly a greater fondness for the Arab, Sidi Hamet, who was kind to Captain Riley and kept his brother Seid from ill-treating him whenever he could. Probably the boy liked him better because the Arab was more picturesque than the Englishman. The whole narrative was very interesting; it had a vein of sincere and earnest piety in it which was not its least charm, and it was written in a style of old-fashioned stateliness which was not without its effect with the boys. [Pg 176]

Somehow they did not think of the Arabs in this narrative as of the same race and faith with the Arabs of Bagdad and the other places in the *Arabian Nights*. They did not think whether these were Mohammedans or not; they naturalized them in the fairy world where all boys are citizens, and lived with them there upon the same familiar terms as they lived with Robinson Crusoe. Their father once told them that *Robinson Crusoe* had robbed the real narrative of Alexander Selkirk of the place it ought to have held in the remembrance of the world; and my boy had a feeling of guilt in reading it, as if he were making himself the accomplice of an impostor.

He liked the *Arabian Nights*, but oddly enough these wonderful tales made no such impression on his fancy as the stories in a wretchedly inferior book made. He did not know the name of this book, or who wrote it; from which I imagine that much of his reading was of the purblind sort that ignorant grown-up people do, without any sort of literary vision. He read this book perpetually, when he was not reading his *Greek and Roman Mythology*; and then suddenly, one day, as happens in childhood with so many things, it vanished out of his possession as if by magic. Perhaps he lost it; perhaps he lent it; at any rate it was gone, and he never got it back, and he never knew what [Pg 177] book it was till thirty years afterward, when he picked up from a friend's library-table a copy of *Gesta Romanorum*, and recognized in this collection of old monkish legends the long-missing treasure of his boyhood.

These stories, without beauty of invention, without art of construction or character, without spirituality in their crude materialization, which were read aloud in the refectories of mediæval cloisters while the monks sat at meat, laid a spell upon the soul of the boy that governed his life. He conformed his conduct to the principles and maxims which actuated the behavior of the shadowy people of these dry-as-dust tales; he went about drunk with the fumes of fables about Roman emperors that never were, in an empire that never was; and, though they tormented him by putting a mixed and impossible civilization in the place of that he knew from his Goldsmith, he was quite helpless to break from their influence. He was always expecting some wonderful thing to happen to him as things happened there in fulfilment of some saying or prophecy; and at every trivial moment he made sayings and prophecies for himself, which he wished events to fulfil. One Sunday when he was walking in an alley behind one of the stores, he found a fur cap that had probably fallen out of the store-loft window. He ran home with it, and [Pg 178] in his simple-hearted rapture he told his mother that as soon as he picked it up there came into his mind the words, "He who picketh up this cap picketh up a fortune," and he could hardly wait for Monday to come and let him restore the cap to its owner and receive an enduring prosperity in reward of his virtue. Heaven knows what form he expected this to take; but when he found himself in the store, he lost all courage; his tongue clove to the roof of his mouth, and he could not utter a syllable of the fine phrases he had made to himself. He laid the cap on the counter without a word; the storekeeper came up and took it in his hand. "What's this?" he said. "Why, this is ours," and he tossed the cap into a loose pile of hats by the showcase, and the boy slunk out, cut to the heart and crushed to the dust. It was such a cruel disappointment and mortification that it was rather a relief to have his brother mock him, and come up and say from time to time, "He who picketh up this cap picketh up a fortune," and then split into a jeering laugh. At least he could fight his brother, and, when he ran, could stone him; and he could throw quads and quoins, and pieces of riglet at the jour printers when the story spread to them, and one of them would begin, "He who picketh— "

He could not make anything either of Byron or Cowper; and he did not even try to read the [Pg 179] little tree-calf volumes of Homer and Virgil which his father had in the versions of Pope and Dryden; the small copper-plates with which they were illustrated conveyed no suggestion to him. Afterward he read Goldsmith's *Deserted Village*, and he formed a great passion for Pope's *Pastorals*, which he imitated in their easy heroics; but till he came to read Longfellow, and Tennyson, and Heine, he never read any long poem without more fatigue than pleasure. His father used to say that the taste for poetry was an acquired taste, like the taste for tomatoes, and that he would come to it yet; but he never came to it, or so much of it as some people seemed to do, and he always had his sorrowful misgivings as to whether they liked it as much as they pretended. I think, too, that it should be a flavor, a spice, a sweet, a delicate relish in the high banquet of literature, and never a chief dish; and I should not know how to defend my boy for trying to make long poems of his own at the very time when he found it so hard to read other people's long poems.

[Pg 181]

V

THE LAST OF A BOY'S TOWN

[Pg 183]

THE LAST OF A BOY'S TOWN

My boy was twelve years old, and was already a swift compositor, though he was still so small that he had to stand on a chair to reach the case in setting type on Taylor's inaugural message. But what he lacked in stature he made up in gravity of demeanor; and he got the name of "The Old Man" from the printers as soon as he began to come about the office, which he did almost as soon as he could walk. His first attempt in literature, an essay on the vain and disappointing nature of human life, he set up and printed off himself in his sixth or seventh year; and the printing-office was in some sort his home, as well as his school, his university. He could no more remember learning to set type than he could remember learning to read; and in after-life he could not come within smell of the ink, the dusty types, the humid paper, of a printing-office without that tender swelling of the heart which so fondly responds to any memory-bearing perfume: his youth, his boyhood, almost his infancy came back to him in it. He now looked forward eagerly [Pg 184] to helping on the new paper, and somewhat proudly to living in the larger place the family were going to. The moment it was decided he began to tell the boys that he was going to live in a city, and he felt that it gave him distinction. He had nothing but joy in it, and he did not dream that as the time drew near it could be sorrow. But when it came at last, and he was to leave the house, the town, the boys, he found himself deathly homesick.

The parting days were days of gloom; the parting was an anguish of bitter tears. Nothing consoled him but the fact that they were going all the way to the new place in a canal-boat, which his father chartered for the trip. My boy and his brother had once gone to Cincinnati in a canal-boat, with a friendly captain of their acquaintance, and, though they were both put to sleep in a berth so narrow that when they turned they fell out on the floor, the glory of the adventure remained with him, and he could have thought of nothing more delightful than such another voyage. The household goods were piled up in the middle of the boat, and the family had a cabin forward, which seemed immense to the children. They played in it and ran races up and down the long canal-boat roof, where their father and mother sometimes put their chairs and sat to admire the scenery. [Pg 185]

They arrived safely at their journey's end, without any sort of accident. They had made the whole forty miles in less than two days, and were all as well as when they started, without having suffered for a moment from seasickness. The boat drew up at the tow-path just before the stable belonging to the house which the father had already taken, and the whole family at once began helping the crew put the things ashore. The boys thought it would have been a splendid stable to keep the pony in, only they had sold the pony; but they saw in an instant that it would do for a circus as soon as they could get acquainted with enough boys to have one.

The strangeness of the house and street, and the necessity of meeting the boys of the neighborhood, and paying with his person for his standing among them, kept my boy interested for a time, and he did not realize at first how much he missed the Boy's Town and all the familiar fellowships there, and all the manifold privileges of the place. Then he began to be very homesick, and to be torn with the torment of a divided love. His mother, whom he loved so dearly, so tenderly, was here, and wherever she was, that was home; and yet home was yonder, far off, at the end of those forty inexorable miles, where he had left his life-long mates. The first months [Pg 186] there was a dumb heartache at the bottom of every pleasure and excitement.

After a while he was allowed to revisit the Boy's Town. It could only have been three or four months after he had left it, but it already seemed a very long time; and he figured himself returning as stage heroes do to the scenes of their childhood, after an absence of some fifteen years. He fancied that if the boys did not find him grown, they would find him somehow changed, and that he would dazzle them with the light accumulated by his residence in a city. He was going to stay with his grandmother, and he planned to make a long stay; for he was very fond of her, and he liked the quiet and comfort of her pleasant house. He must have gone back by the canal-packet, but his memory kept no record of the fact, and afterward he knew only of having arrived, and of searching about in a ghostly fashion for his old comrades. They may have been at school; at any rate, he found very few of them; and with them he was certainly strange enough; too strange, even. They received him with a kind of surprise; and they could not begin playing together at once in the old way. He went to all the places that were so dear to him; but he felt in them the same kind of refusal, or reluctance, that he felt in the boys. His heart began to ache again, he did not quite know why; only [Pg 187] it ached. When he went up from his grandmother's to look at the Faulkner house, he realized that it was no longer home, and he could not bear the sight of it. There were other people living in it; strange voices sounded from the open doors, strange faces peered from the windows.

He came back to his grandmother's, bruised and defeated, and spent the morning indoors reading. After dinner he went out again, and hunted up that queer earth-spirit who had been so long and closely his only friend. He at least was not changed; he was as unwashed and as unkempt as ever; but he seemed shy of my poor boy. He had probably never been shaken hands with in his life before; he dropped my boy's hand; and they stood looking at each other, not knowing what to say. My boy had on his best clothes, which he wore so as to affect the Boy's Town boys with the full splendor of a city boy. After all, he was not so very splendid, but his presence altogether was too much for the earth-spirit, and he vanished out of his consciousness like an apparition.

After school was out in the afternoon, he met more of the boys, but none of them knew just what to do with him. The place that he had once had in their lives was filled; he was an outsider, who might be suffered among them, but [Pg 188] he was no longer of them. He did not understand this at once, nor well know what hurt him. But something was gone that could not be called back, something lost that could not be found.

At tea-time his grandfather came home and gravely made him welcome; the uncle who was staying with them was jovially kind. But a heavy homesickness weighed down the child's heart, which now turned from the Boy's Town as longingly as it had turned toward it before.

They all knelt down with the grandfather before they went to the table. There had been a good many deaths from cholera during the day, and the grandfather prayed for grace and help amid the pestilence that walketh in darkness and wasteth at noonday in such a way that the boy felt there would be very little of either for him unless he got home at once. All through the meal that followed he was trying to find the courage to say that he must go home. When he managed to say it, his grandmother and aunt tried to comfort and coax him, and his uncle tried to shame him, out of his homesickness, to joke it off, to make him laugh. But his grandfather's tender heart was moved. He could not endure the child's mute misery; he said he must go home if he wished.

In half an hour the boy was on the canal-packet speeding homeward at the highest pace of the [Pg 189] three-horse team, and the Boy's Town was out of sight. He could not sleep for excitement that night, and he came and spent the time talking on quite equal terms with the steersman, one of the canalers whom he had admired afar in earlier and simpler days. He found him a very amiable fellow, by no means haughty, who began to tell him funny stories, and who even let him take the helm for a while. The rudder-handle was of polished iron, very different from the clumsy wooden affair of a freight-boat; and the packet made in a single night the distance which the boy's family had been nearly two days in travelling when they moved away from the Boy's Town.

He arrived home for breakfast a travelled and experienced person, and wholly cured of that longing for his former home that had tormented him before he revisited its scenes. He now fully gave himself up to his new environment, and looked forward and not backward. I do not mean to say that he ceased to love the Boy's Town; that he could not do and never did. But he became more and more aware that the past was gone from him forever, and that he could not return to it. He did not forget it, but cherished its memories the more fondly for that reason.

There was no bitterness in it, and no harm that he could not hope would easily be forgiven him. He had often been foolish, and sometimes [Pg 190] he had been wicked; but he had never been such a little fool or such a little sinner but he had wished for more sense and more grace. There are some great fools and great sinners who try to believe in after-life that they are the manlier men because they have been silly and mischievous boys, but he has never believed that. He is glad to have had a boyhood fully rounded out with all a boy's interests and pleasures, and he is glad that his lines were cast in the Boy's Town; but he knows, or believes he knows, that whatever is good in him now came from what was good in him then; and he is sure that the town was delightful chiefly because his home in it was happy. The town was small, and the boys there were hemmed in by their inexperience and ignorance; but the simple home was large with vistas that stretched to the ends of the earth, and it was serenely bright with a father's reason and warm with a mother's love.

THE END